I0654767

Abijah Fowler, Josiah Fowler

The Southern School Arithmetic

Youth's assistant - containing the most concise and accurate rules for performing

operations in arithmetic, adapted to the easy and regular instruction of youth, for

the use of schools

Abijah Fowler, Josiah Fowler

The Southern School Arithmetic
Youth's assistant - containing the most concise and accurate rules for performing operations in arithmetic, adapted to the easy and regular instruction of youth, for the use of schools

ISBN/EAN: 9783337390839

Printed in Europe, USA, Canada, Australia, Japan

Cover: Foto ©Andreas Hilbeck / pixelio.de

More available books at **www.hansebooks.com**

THE
SOUTHERN SCHOOL ARITHMETIC;

OR,

YOUTH'S ASSISTANT.

CONTAINING

THE MOST CONCISE AND ACCURATE RULES FOR
PERFORMING OPERATIONS IN

ARITHMETIC,

ADAPTED TO THE EASY AND REGULAR INSTRUCTION OF YOUTH,

FOR THE USE OF SCHOOLS, &c.

By A. & J. FOWLER,
TEACHERS OF ARITHMETIC.

REVISED BY M. GIBSON

TO WHICH IS ANNEXED AN APPENDIX, CONTAINING

MENSURATION OF SURFACES, TABLES OF FOREIGN MONEY,
AND BOOK-KEEPING.

STEREOTYPE EDITION.

RICHMOND:
WEST & JOHNSTON, 145 MAIN STREET.
1864.

ENTERED according to act of Congress, in the year 1834, by ABIJAH & JOSIAH FOWLER, in the Clerk's Office for the Eastern District of Tennessee, at Knoxville.

RE-ENTERED according to act of Congress, in the year 1850, by L. GIFFORD, in the Clerk's Office for the Eastern District of Tennessee, of Knoxville.

RE-ENTERED according to act of Congress, in the year 1864, by WEST & JOHNSTON, in the Clerk's Office, for the Eastern District of Virginia, at Richmond.

RECOMMENDATIONS.

MESSRS. FOWLERS' ARITHMETIC.

This work, which was handed me some time since, for examination, exhibits a degree of industry and ability highly creditable to the authors. The order of arrangement appears to be judicious, and the illustrations clear and plain. The circumstance that it is primarily adapted to our national currency, is, to me, one of its chief recommendations; and were no works of an opposite character introduced into our common schools, we should soon have a currency or mode of reckoning, simple, uniform, and intelligible to every one. I trust the gentlemen will meet with such encouragement from the public, as will more than compensate for the trouble and expense of publication.   JOSEPH ESTABROOK,
            President of the East Tennessee College.
Knoxville, April 29th, 1834.

MESSRS. FOWLERS' ARITHMETIC.

From a hasty examination of this work, I would say, its judicious arrangement, the perspicuity and conciseness of its rules, the clearness and simplicity of its illustrations, and its adaptation to our national currency, render it a desirable companion for the beginning in this important branch of education. I trust the industry and ability exhibited by its youthful authors, will meet with liberal encouragement.
                    ALLEN H. MATHES,
            Late Principal of the Male Academy.
Madisonville, June 14th, 1834.

THE FEDERAL INSTRUCTOR; OR, YOUTHS' ASSISTANT.

The above work, in my opinion, has considerable merit. The rules appear to me, to be made plain to the understanding of beginners, and unadvanced learners, in the very useful branch of knowledge on which it treats. Hope is entertained that Messrs. Fowlers', the authors of it, will be liberally rewarded for their undertaking, by the patronage of a generous public.
                    HENRY C. SAFFELL,
            Principal of the Holston Seminary.
New-Market, June 26th, 1835.

Having carefully examined "FOWLERS' ARITHMETIC," I make no hesitation in saying that I fully concur with the foregoing gentlemen in opinion, with respect to the merits of the work, and cordially unite with them in recommending its introduction into our schools and academies, as well as particularly into the Tyro's Library.

JOSIAH P. SMITH, Philom.

Kingston, Oct., 1836.

———

MESSRS. FOWLERS:

I have carefully examined your Arithmetic, and must say, after twenty-five years experience as a teacher, that I have not seen a work of the kind that I would prefer before it, especially for young beginners. The shortness, simplicity, and plainness of the rules, as you have very justly remarked in your preface, must I think greatly accelerate the progress of learners. I trust you will meet with the patronage of our fellow-citizens generally.

LANDON DUNCAN.

, Giles County, Virginia, March 15th, 1836.

———

MESSRS. FOWLERS:

Gentlemen—I have carefully examined your treatise on Arithmetic, and I think it superior to any other now in use to facilitate the progress of the young learner, and is fully adequate for all the common business of our country. It well merits a place in our schools and Academies, as well as in our houses.

MICHAEL MORRIS,
Teacher of the Estillville Academy.

Estillville, Va., 13th July, 1836.

EXPLANATION OF CHARACTERS, SIGNS AND SIGNIFICATIONS.

$=$ Equal, as 100 cts. $= $1.$

$+$ More, as $4 + 2 = 6.$

$-$ Less, as $6 - 2 = 4.$

$\times$ Into, with, or multiplied by, as $4 \times 2 = 8.$

$\div$ By, i. e. divided by, as $6 \div 2 = 3.$ or 2)6(3.

$:::$ Proportion, as $2 : 4 :: 6 : 12.$

$\sqrt{}$ Square Root, as $\sqrt{64} = 8.$

$\sqrt[3]{}$ Cube Root, as $\sqrt[3]{64} = 4.$

$\sqrt[4]{}$ Fourth Root, as $\sqrt[4]{16} = 2$, &c.

PREFACE.

THE design of the authors in bringing this work before the public is, to teach the science of ARITHMETIC in a different and easier manner than has been customary. To attain this object, we have simplified the necessary rules, thus leading the student out of the darkness of ignorance by a plain path, into the light of knowledge. The shortness, simplicity and plainness of the rules, will enable the student to advance with greater ease and speed than those hitherto promulged.

As calculating in English money is measurably obsolete, the authors have, with but few exceptions, employed, in this work, the legal currency of our country, DOLLARS and CENTS. Two things among us have been but too well fitted to retard the progress of Arithmetical knowledge; calculations in *pounds, shillings, pence* and *farthings*, a currency unknown among us, and unsuited to the transactions of our common country concerns; and long, complex rules, difficult to be remembered, and still more difficult to comprehend. But, make your rules short, familiar, and easy to be understood, and the student is encouraged to pursue the shining path of science, thus plainly pointed out to him with alacrity and delight.

Though this work may appear short, yet there are in it 1300 questions, or upwards—a sufficiency, we should think, in point of number; selected so as to be useful, and adapted to the circumstances of our country.

Many persons who have ciphered for months, and some who have gone through the Arithmetic, are at a loss because they do not understand, or have not paid attention to the rules. This evil will be the more easily remedied on our system, as our rules are plain and short, and may, with but little labour, be committed to memory.

When our Saviour came into the world, he was condemned by the Jews by asking a simple question—*can any thing good come out of Nazareth?* If any are disposed, in a similar way, to denounce our work, we would beg of them to examine carefully and candidly before they decide, and to remember, that, as the Messiah did come out of Nazareth, so, it is possible for a good Arithmetic to be made in Tennessee. We are, indeed, devotedly attached to this study, and as we think we have made improvements in the mode of teaching it, we have risked our all to give publicity to the book, to enable others to judge of it and to profit by it.

CONTENTS.

ARITHMETIC.

ARITHMETIC is that part of the Mathematics which teaches the art of computation by numbers. All operations in Arithmetic are performed by means of the following figures, viz: One 1, two 2, three 3, four 4, five 5, six 6, seven 7, eight 8, nine 9, cipher 0.

NUMERATION.

NUMERATION teaches the different value of figures by their different places, and to express any proposed numbers either by words or characters; or to read and write any sum or number.

NUMERATION TABLE.

Hundreds of Millions	Tens of Millions	Millions	Hundreds of Thousands	Tens of Thousands	Thousands	Hundreds	Tens	Units	
								1	One.
							2	1	Twenty-one.
						3	2	1	Three hundred 21.
					4	3	2	1	Four thousand 321.
				5	4	3	2	1	54 thousand 321.
			6	5	4	3	2	1	654 thousand 321.
		7	6	5	4	3	2	1	7 million 654 thousand 321.
	8	7	6	5	4	3	2	1	87 million 654 thousand 321.
9	8	7	6	5	4	3	2	1	987 million 654 thousand 321.

The preceding contains only nine digits, which render it sufficiently large for young students or common business, although it may be extended much farther, thus:

Quintillions.	Quatrillions.	Trillions.	Billions.	Millions.	Units.
987,654;	327,241;	278,325;	256,148;	212,563;	652,324.

ADDITION`

The use of Addition is to ascertain the amount of two or more numbers when put together.

RULE.

1st. Set down any one of the numbers and place under it all the rest in such a manner that units may stand under units, tens under tens, hundreds under hundreds, and so on, and draw a line under the last.

2d. Begin at the right hand column and add together all the figures contained in that column. If it amounts to ten or more, set down the right hand figure and carry the left hand figure or figures, which add to the next line, and so proceed till adding the last line. Then set down the whole amount.

EXAMPLES.

(No. 1.)	(2.)	(3.)	(4.)	(5.)
Units	Units Tens.	Units Tens. Hundreds.	Units Tens. Hundreds. Thousands	Units Tens. Hundreds. Thousands
4	5 3	2 3 4	1 3 4 6	2 4 6 8
4	4 1	1 2 1	7 2 1 2	1 7 5 5
2	6 9	4 6 8	1 0 3 2	1 0 2 0
2	2 5	2 2 4	8 1 0 3	1 2 8 0
Ans. 12	1 8 8	1 0 4 7	1 7 6 9 3	6 5 2 3

(6.)	(7.)	(8.)	(9.)
1 2 3	2 4 6 8	8 7 5 6 1	4 2 1 4 6
4 2 2	6 2 7 3	1 0 4 2 0	2 3 3 2 3
5 3 1	2 1 0 3	3 2 6 1 9	1 3 3 5 7
2 4 6	4 3 1 2	3 1 4 2 7	2 4 5 5 7
3 2 3	3 1 0 2	6 1 4 2 2	1 2 7 8 7
1 6 4 5	1 8 2 5 8	2 2 3 4 4 9	1 1 6 1 7 0

(10.)	(11.)	(12.)
2 2	2 5 6 3 1 2	4 6 2 1
4 1 0	3 0 1 9 1	2 3 0 0
1 1 2 2 4	4 3 0 7	9 6 1 3 1
2 4 7 9 5	7 7 9	1 2 0 0 1 2
3 6 1 3 5	2 4 0 2	1 2
8 7 2 8 2	1 2 4 8 0 0	9 0 0
1 5 9 8 6 8	4 1 8 7 9 1	2 2 3 9 7 6

13. Add the following numbers, viz: 14, 16, 23, 29, 80, 31, and 100, and tell their amount.   Ans. 293.

14. What is the amount of 36, 97, 125, 384, 1176?   Ans. 1818.

15. Add 640, 79, 80, 100, 210, 450, 787, 21, and 2.   Ans. 2369.

16. John gave Joseph 33 apples; James gave him 91; Peter gave him 56; Joel gave him 107; and David gave him 95; how many had he?   Ans. 382.

17. A person went to collect money, and received of one man $542; of another 654; of another 550; of another 787, and of another 3405. I demand the sum collected. Ans. 5938.

18. John owes to one man $302; to another 540; to another 70; to another 2356, and to another 999. How much does he owe in all?   Ans. $4267

19. John and Charles went to collect nuts; when they had collected a quantity, sat down to count them; when one had collected 275 and the other 196, what number did both of them collect?   Ans. 471.

20. Desired to purchase a suit of clothes which cost as follows, viz: a coat $25, a pair of pantaloons 10, a waistcoat 6, a shirt 2, and a pair of socks 1. What is the cost of the whole?   Ans. $44.

21. A butcher bought of one man 25 head of cattle; of

another 15; of another 40, and of another 9. How many did he buy in all? Ans. 89 head.

22. A man in buying cider received of one man 90 gallons; of another 200; of another 300; of another 400, and of another 500. How many gallons did he buy in all?
Ans. 1490.

23. A gentleman went to purchase brandy, and bought of one man 125 gallons; of another 160; of another 190, and of another 210. How much did he buy in all?
Ans. 685 gallons.

24. A man in buying corn, received of one person 400 bushels; of another 500; of another 600, and of another 700. How many bushels did he buy in all? Ans. 2200 bushels.

MULTIPLICATION.

When the multiplier does not exceed 12, work by

RULE I.

Set the multiplier under the right hand figure or figures of the multiplicand: then beginning with the units, multiply all the figures of the multiplicand in succession, and set down the several products; but if either of the products be more than 9, set down its right hand figure only, and add its left hand figure or figures to the next product. The whole of the last product must be set down.

PROOF. Divide the answer by the multiplier, and the quotient will equal the given sum.

MULTIPLICATION TABLE.

The learner should commit the following table to memory before he proceeds further:

Twice		3 times		4 times		5 times		6 times		7 times	
1 make 2		1 make 3		1 make 4		1 make 5		1 make 6		1 make 7	
2	4	2	6	2	8	2	10	2	12	2	14
3	6	3	9	3	12	3	15	3	18	3	21
4	8	4	12	4	16	4	20	4	24	4	28
5	10	5	15	5	20	5	25	5	30	5	35
6	12	6	18	6	24	6	30	6	36	6	42
7	14	7	21	7	28	7	35	7	42	7	49
8	16	8	24	8	32	8	40	8	48	8	56
9	18	9	27	9	36	9	45	9	54	9	63
10	20	10	30	10	40	10	50	10	60	10	70
11	22	11	33	11	44	11	55	11	66	11	77
12	24	12	36	12	48	12	60	12	72	12	84

8 times		9 times		10 times		11 times		12 times	
1 make 8		1 make 9		1 make 10		1 make 11		1 make 12	
2	16	2	18	2	20	2	22	2	24
3	24	3	27	3	30	3	33	3	36
4	32	4	36	4	40	4	44	4	48
5	40	5	45	5	50	5	55	5	60
6	48	6	54	6	60	6	66	6	72
7	56	7	63	7	70	7	77	7	84
8	64	8	72	8	80	8	88	8	96
9	72	9	81	9	90	9	99	9	108
10	80	10	90	10	100	10	110	10	120
11	88	11	99	11	110	11	121	11	132
12	96	12	108	12	120	12	132	12	144

(1.) 412 multiplicand.
  2 multiplier.

  824 product.

(2.) 5498
  3

Ans. 16494

(3.) 12347
  4

Ans. 49388

(4.) 12349172
  5

61745860

(5.) 98754
  6

592524

(6.) 12345678910
  7

86419752370

(7.) 64115928
  8

512927424

(8.) 21988
  9

197442

(9.) 98765432144
  10

987654321440

(10.) 5324786
  11

Ans. 58572646

(11.) 84532911
  12

Ans. 1014394932

(12.) 1481000763
  3

Ans. 4443002289

(13.) 150000000000
  2

Ans. 300000000000

(14.) 110008191
  4

Ans. 440032764

(15.) 987554321
  2

Ans. 1975108642

(16.) 17853440
  5

Ans. 89267200

(17.) 1888880000
  5

Ans. 9444400000

(18.) 1280721
　　　　　　3
Ans. 3692163

(19.) 9922446688
　　　　　　　4
Ans. 39689786752

(20.) 60011500843211
　　　　　　　　　7
Ans. 420080505902477

21.	Multiply	21141	by	2	Answer	42282
22.		73211	,	3	.. ...	219633
23.	... ;	87692	...'	4	. . ...	350768
24.	.	95698	..	5	... ...	478490
25.	..	91144	'	6	....	546864
26. ..	.	83456	.	7	....	584192
27. .	..	21110	....	8	.. ....	168880
28.	. ..	34000	...	9	......	306000
29.	. ..	10056	... .10		....	100560
30.	...	20000	11		....	220000
31.	.	.800510	..12		.... .	.9606120

When the multiplier exceeds 12, work by

RULE II.

Multiply by each figure separately. First by the one at the right hand, then by the next, and so on, placing their respective products one under another, with the right hand figure of each product directly under that figure of the multiplier by which it is produced. Add these products together, and their amount will be the answer.

EXAMPLES.

(32.) 120 multiplicand.
　　　14 multiplier.
　　　────
　　　480
　　　120
　　　────
Ans. 1680

(33.) 1451
　　　　16
　　　────
　　8706
　　1451
　　────
Ans. 23216

| (34.) | 124680 | | (35.) | 468 |
| | 142 | | | 72 |

249360		936
498720		3276
124680		
		33696
17704560		

36. Multiply 4875 by 29 Answer 141375
37 ... .11271 ... .35....... .394185
38 .. .19004 ....305. 5796220
39. ..... .76976 .....489.......37641264
40. ....84769 ....976.. 82734544
41 ... .1978987 ...4809 9516948483

Note. When there are ciphers at the right of either the multiplicand or multiplier, multiply as in the preceding case, only omitting the ciphers. Then add together the several products, and place to the right of the amount as many ciphers as are to the right of both factors.

EXAMPLES.

(42.) Multiply 400 by 200 Answer 80000
200

80000

43. .8000.... ..400. .3200000
44 .3700 .200. . 740000
45. ..4870 ....2500. 12175000
46. .876956. .990000. .868186440000

Note. When the multiplier exceeds 12, and is the exact product of any 2 factors in the multiplication table, the operation may be performed thus:—Multiply the given sum by one of said factors, and that product by the other factor.

EXAMPLES.

(47.) Multiply 2851 by 15 3 times 5 are 15
3

8553
5

Ans. 42765

48.	Multiply	476	by	25	Answer	11900
49.	..	7696.		.81.	....	.623376
50	..	.8976.		.48	......	.430848
51.	...	.87698.	..	...72	....	.6314256
52.	.. ...	.20784.		.108	....	.2244672
53	....	.81207	..·.	.132	.....	10719324
54.	...	.47696.		.144	.. ....,	6868224
55.	.... .	75687	.	.56.	....	4238472
56.	....	34075	.....	..36	....	1226700

PRACTICAL EXAMPLES.

57. A man has 25 stables, and in each stable there are five horses, how many has he in all?   Ans. 125.

58. A man has four chests, and in each chest there are four dollars, how many dollars are there in all?   Ans. 16.

59. Josiah has 30 apples, and James has six times that number, how many has James?   Ans. 180.

60. A man has three tracts of land, each containing 52 acres, how many acres has he in all?   Ans. 156.

61. A laborer hired himself for six years, at $75 per year, how much did he receive for the six years' labor? Ans. $450.

62. A certain potato field is 90 hills in length, and breadth 100, how many hills are there in the field?   Ans. 9000.

63. A certain cornfield is 98 hills in length, and 10 in breadth, how many hills are there in the field?   Ans. 980.

64. A man having built a house, found he had used 18,175 bricks, how many bricks will be necessary to build 14 houses of the same size?   Ans. 254450.

SUBTRACTION.

Subtraction is used to know the difference between a larger and smaller number.

RULE.

Set down the larger number first, and under it with units under units, tens under tens, the smaller. Then begin at the right hand or unit's place, and take the lower figure from the one above it, if the upper figure be more than the lower, and set down the remainder. But if the upper figure be less than the lower, add 10 to the upper figure, take the lower figure from the amount, set down the remainder, and carry one to the next lower figure.

PROOF. Add the lower number and the answer together, and their amount will equal the upper.

EXAMPLES.

(1.) From 964   (2.) 841
      Take 333   579
      ___   ___
      Ans. 631   Ans. 262

 3. From 487   Take 96   Ans. 391
 4.   875   302   573
 5.   967   351   616
 6.   1001   487   514
 7.   9765   1307   8458
 8.   87696   10091   77605
 9.   455692   300120   155572
10.   1000000   1   999999
11.   10000   9   9991

12. James has 44 apples, and John 24. How many more has James than John?   Ans. 20.

13. Henry has 25 marbles, and Charles 8. How many more has Henry than Charles?   Ans. 17.

14. William holds Jesse's note for $99. He has now paid $37 How much does he still owe?   Ans. $62.

15. A merchant had $1000, but has lent 105. How much has he left?   Ans. $895.

16. I owe $560. After I pay $69, how much will I still owe?   Ans. $491.

17. A merchant had 180 yards of cloth, but sold 75. How many had he left?   Ans. 105 yds.

18. A farmer had 999 acres of land, but has given his son 500. How much has he left?   Ans. 499 acres.

19. There are two piles of bricks. In the greater pile there are 7896, and in the less 4389. How many more are there in the greater pile than in the less?   Ans. 3507.

20. A merchant bought 4875 bushels of wheat, out of which he sold 2976 bushels. How many bushels had he left?   Ans. 1899 bushels.

21. I deposited in bank $1240. I have since taken out $1082. How much remains?   Ans. $158.

22. A farmer had 5487 acres of land. He sold to A 325, to B 750, and to C 1000 acres. How many had he left?   Ans. 3412 acres.

2*

23. I had 1200 pounds of pork, and sold to one man 400, to another 350, and to another 125. How much was left?
               Ans. 325.

24. In a certain milk house there were 44 crocks of milk, but it so happened an unruly cat broke in and destroyed 19. How many were left?   Ans. 25.

25. In a certain barrel are 94 gallons of wine. If 20 be drawn out, how many will be left?   Ans. 74.

26. A ship's crew consisted of 75 men, 21 of whom died at sea. How many arrived safe in port? Ans. 54.

27. A tree had 647 apples on it, but 158 of them fell off. How many were there then remaining on the tree?
               Ans. 489.

28. I saw 15 ladies; 8 returned back. How many passed on?   Ans. 7.

29. A general had an army of 43250 men; 15342 of them deserted. How many remained?   Ans. 27908.

30. A man starting a journey of 950 miles. When he may have gone 348 miles, how far has he still to go?
             Ans. 602 miles.

31. A trader had 655 hogs; 99 of them were stolen; 24 died of sickness; he then sold 400. How many had he left?   Ans. 132.

SHORT DIVISION.

By Division we ascertain how often one number is contained in another. The number to be divided is called the dividend. The number to divide by is called the divisor. The number of times the dividend contains the divisor is called the quotient. If on dividing there be a remainder it is called the overplus.

RULE.

Place the divisor to the left of the number you wish to divide. Consider how many times the number by which you wish to divide is contained in the first figure or figures of the number to be divided, and set down the result, noting whether there be any remainder. If there be no remainder, consider how often the divisor is contained in the next figure or figures; but if there be a remainder, conceive it to be placed to the left of the next figure; into which divide as before, and set down the result.

PROOF. Multiply the quotient by the divisor; add in the remainder, if any. The product will equal the dividend.

EXAMPLES.

(1.) Divide 336 by 3
   3)336

   Ans. 112

(2.) Divide 448 by 2
   2)448

   Ans. 224

(3.) 2)4681278

   2340639

(4.) 3)63912964

   21304321

(5.) 4)1896431

   474107 + 3

(6.) 5)863200

   172640

(7.) 6)9654630

   1609105

(8.) 7)1269503450

   181357635 + 5

9.	Divide	8767	by	5	Answer	1753	+ 2
10.	—	9698	—	6	—	1616	+ 2
11.	—	97899	—	7	—	13985	+ 4
12.	—	80409	—	8	—	10051	+ 1
13.	—	981021	—	9	—	109002	+ 3
14.	—	897697	—	10	—	89769	+ 7
15.	—	9876978	—	11	—	897907	+ 1
16.	—	4967844	—	12	—	413987	

17. Divide 336 pounds of sugar equally among 3 boys?
Ans. 112.

18. Divide 1284 pounds of cotton equally among 4 girls?
Ans. 321.

19. Divide 8655 acres of land equally between 2 heirs?
Ans. 4327.

20 Bought 6 horses for 318 dollars. How much did each cost?
Ans. 53 dollars.

21. John would divide 120 ears of corn among 10 horses. What was the share of each?
Ans. 12.

22. Divide 1260 pounds of coffee among 12 women?
Ans. 105.

23. I would divide 8880 apples among 8 boys. What was the share of each?
Ans. 1110.

LONG DIVISION.

Long Division is used when the divisor exceeds 12.

RULE.

Place the divisor to the left of the dividend, as in short division. Consider how often the divisor is contained in the least number of figures into which it can be divided, and set down the result to the right of the dividend. Multiply the figures set at the right of the dividend by the divisor, and set the product under the figure in which you considered how often the divisor was contained. Subtract the product from the line above it, and set down what remains, which must always be less than the divisor. Bring down the next figure to the right of the remainder, and proceed as before, till all the figures of the dividend are brought down. When there are ciphers at the right of both factors, the operation may be shortened by cutting off an equal number of ciphers from each.

EXAMPLES.

(1.)   Divisor   24)480 dividend.   Ans. 20.

$$48$$
$$\overline{}$$
$$0$$

(2.)   25)450   Ans. 18.

$$25$$
$$\overline{}$$
$$200$$
$$200$$
$$\overline{}$$

		by		Ans.		Remainder
3.	Divide 456	by 21	Ans.	21	Remainder	15
4.	361	19		19		
5.	958	18		53		4
6.	12350	15		823		5
7.	1475	28		52		19
8.	4277	31		137		30
9.	25757	37		696		5
10.	256976	41		6267		29
11.	997816	59		16912		8
12.	4697680424	125		37581443		49
13.	9924000	54000		183		42
14.	74000000	3700		20000		

15. Divide 80906000   by   180 Ans. 449477 Remainder 14
16.   555555555   55555   10000   5555
17.   3875642   7898   490   5622
18.   98765432   1234   80086   1008
19.   12486240   87654   142   39372
20.   57289761   7569   7569
21.   99607765   27000   3689   4765
22.   15463420   1600   9664   1020

PRACTICAL EXAMPLES.

23. If 1860 pounds of beef be divided equally among 60 men, what will be the share of each?   Ans. 31 pounds.

24. 4556 pounds of salt are to be equally divided among an army of 44 men. What will be the share of each man? Ans. 103 + 24.

25. 4006 pounds of malt are to be divided equally among an army of 84 men. What will be the share of each man? Ans. 47 + 58.

26. 1600 bushels of corn are to be divided equally among 40 men, how much is that a piece?   Ans. 40.

27. A regiment consisting of 500 men are allowed 1000 pounds of pork per day. How much is each man's part? Ans. 2 lb.

28. If a field of 32 acres produce 1920 bushels of corn, how much is that per acre?   Ans. 60 bushels.

29. A prize of $25526 is to be equally divided among 100 men. What will be each man's part? Ans. $255 + 26.

30. How many horses, at $30 per head, may be bought for $38040?   Ans. 1268.

31. If a field containing 25 acres produces 375 bushels of wheat, how much does one acre produce? Ans. 15 bushels.

32. 96 persons are to have 480 pounds of beef divided equally among them. What is the share of each? Ans. 5 pounds.

33. 144 men are to pay equal shares of a debt which amounts to $144000. How much must each man advance to make up the sum?   Ans. $100.

34. If $2400 be equally divided among 16 persons, what will be the share of each?   Ans. $150.

35. A man gave 35 reapers $385, each to have an equal part. How much did each man receive?   Ans. $11.

36. A man travelled 560 miles in 40 days. How far was that in one day?   Ans. 14 miles.

37. A boy hired 60 days, for which he was to receive $120. How much was one day's labor worth?   Ans. $2.

38. When I have labored 60 days for the sum of $180, how much is one day's labor worth at that rate?   Ans. $3.

EXAMPLES TO TRY THE STUDENT IN ORDER THAT HE MAY UNDERSTAND THE FOREGOING RULES, VIZ: ADDITION, MULTIPLICATION, SUBTRACTION AND DIVISION.

39. John had 40 apples. He gave his brother 10; kept 10; and divided the rest equally between his two sisters. How many had each sister?   Ans. 10.

40. John owes James $50. Peter owes him $80. David owes him $105. Samuel $91. Eli $7. And Joseph $40. After James collects the above debts and pays $99, which he owes, how much will he have?   Ans. $274.

41. A farmer has three tracts of land, each containing 20 acres; buys an adjoining one of 90 acres. If he sell 40 acres, and divide the rest equally between his two sons, what will be the share of each?   Ans. 55.

42. A person has 50 sheep; buys from his neighbor 50 more; he then sells 25 to the butcher. How many has he left?   Ans. 75.

43. A gentleman dying left $2500, to be divided as follows: To his son 1500 dollars, and the rest equally between his two daughters. How much did each daughter receive?   Ans. 500 dollars.

44. A person went to collect money, and received of one man 800 dollars; of another 60; of another 18; of another 440, and of another 25. After which, by gambling, he lost 103 dollars. How much had he left?   Ans. 1230 dollars.

45. Suppose a certain field be 140 hills in length, and 124 in breadth. Admit there be two stalks in every hill, and on each stalk an ear of corn, how many bushels are there in the field, suppose 100 ears to make a bushel?   Ans. 347 bushels + 20.

46. Bought 25 yards of fine cloth for 250 dollars. How much was it per yard?   Ans. 10 dollars.

47. Bought 16 loads of hay at 4 dollars per load. What did it amount to?   Ans. 64 dollars.

48. How many yards of cloth, at 6 dollars per yard, can I have for 90 dollars?   Ans. 15 yards.

49. How many pair of gloves, at 1 dollar per pair, can I have for 4 dollars?   Ans. 4.

TABLES

OF MONEY, WEIGHTS, AND MEASURES.

FEDERAL MONEY.

The denominations are,

10 Mills (marked m.) make	1 Cent, ct.
10 Cents	1 Dime, d.
10 Dimes (or 100 cts.)	1 Dollar, D. or $
10 Dollars	1 Eagle, E.

AVOIRDUPOIS WEIGHT.

The denominations are,

16 Drams (marked dr.) make	1 Ounce, oz.
16 Ounces	1 Pound, lb.
28 Pounds	1 Quarter, qr.
4 Quarters (or 112 lbs.)	1 Hundred weight, cwt.
20 Hundred weight	1 Ton, T.

TROY WEIGHT.

The denominations are,

24 Grains make	1 Pennyweight, dwt.
20 Pennyweights	1 Ounce, oz.
12 Ounces	1 Pound, lb.

APOTHECARIES WEIGHT.

The denominations are,

20 Grains (*gr.*) make	1 Scruple, Э
3 Scruples	1 Dram, Ʒ
8 Drams	1 Ounce, Ʒ
12 Ounces	1 Pound, ℔

Note. By Avoirdupois Weight are weighed all things of a coarse, drossy nature; and all metals, but gold or silver, by Troy Weight. Jewels, gold, silver, and liquors, are weighed by Apothecaries Weight. Apothecaries mix their medicine by Troy, but buy and sell by Avoirdupois Weight.

LONG MEASURE.

The denominations are,

12 Inches (*in.*) make	1 Foot,	*ft.*
3 Feet	1 Yard,	*yd.*
5½ Yards (or 16½ feet)	1 Rod, pole, or perch,	*P.*
40 Poles (or 220 yds.)	1 Furlong,	*fur.*
8 Furlongs (or 1760 yds.)	1 Mile,	*M.*
3 Miles	1 League,	*L.*
60 Geographic, or } miles 69½ Statute }	1 Degree,	*deg.*
360 Degrees the circumference of the Earth.		

LAND OR SQUARE MEASURE.

The denominations are,

144 Square inches (*in.*) make	1 Square foot,	*ft.*
9 Square feet	1 Square yard,	*yd.*
30¼ Square yards	1 Rod, pole, or perch,	*P.*
40 Square perches .	1 Rood,	*R.*
4 Roods . .	1 Acre,	*A.*
640 Acres	1 Square Mile, .	*M.*

CLOTH MEASURE.

The denominations are,

2¼ Inches (*in.*) make	1 Nail,	*na.*
4 Nails	1 Quarter of a yard,	*qr.*
4 Quarters . .	1 Yard, . .	*yd.*
3 Quarters . .	1 Ell Flemish,	*E. Fl.*
5 Quarters	1 Ell English,	*E. E.*
6 Quarters . .	1 Ell French,	*E. F.*

LIQUID MEASURE.

The denominations are,

4 Gills (*gi.*) make	1 Pint, .	*pt.*
2 Pints .	1 Quart,	*qt.*
4 Quarts . .	1 Gallon,	*gal.*
31½ Gallons	1 Barrel,	*bar.*
63 Gallons . . .	1 Hogshead,	*hhd.*
2 Hogsheads . .	1 Pipe or butt,	*P.* or *B.*
2 Pipes (252 gal. or 4 hhds.)	1 Ton,	*T.*

DRY MEASURE.

The denominations are,

2 Pints (*pt.*)	make	1 Quart,	*qt.*
8 Quarts .	. . .	1 Peck,	*pe.*
4 Pecks . .	.	1 Bushel,	*bu.*

Note. Long Measure is used for measuring lengths, distances, &c. Land or Square Measure is used for measuring lands, &c. Cloth Measure is used for measuring cloth, tape, &c. Liquid Measure is used for measuring vinegar, rum, brandy, wine, cider, perry, oil, &c. And Dry Measure is used for measuring grain, fruit, salt, &c.

TIME.

The denominations are,

60 Seconds (*sec.*)	make	1 Minute,	*min.*
60 Minutes		1 Hour,	*hr.*
24 Hours	. .	1 Day,	*da.*
7 Days		1 Week,	*w.*
52 Weeks, 1 day and 6 hours, or			
365 Days and 6 hours,	}	1 Year,	*y.*
12 Calender months		1 Year,	*y.*
13 Lunar months .		1 Year,	*y.*

The following is a statement of the number of days in each of the twelve calender months :

Thirty days hath September,
April, June and November ;
All the rest have thirty-one,
Except the second month alone,
Which has but twenty-eight in fine,
Till leap year gives it twenty-nine.

COMPOUND ADDITION.

Compound Addition consists of several denominations.

RULE.

Set the numbers of like denomination under each other, leaving a space between. Then begin at the right hand column, and add, as in Simple Addition. Divide the amount by as many as will make one of the next greater. If there be any remainder, set it down under the column added. If no remainder, set down a cipher. Carry the quotient preduced by dividing, to the next higher denomination, and so proceed.

PROOF. As in Simple Addition.

Note. In adding fractions, count $\frac{1}{4}$ one, $\frac{1}{2}$ two, $\frac{3}{4}$ three, because four fourths make a whole one. Or if thirds, count $\frac{1}{3}$ one, $\frac{2}{3}$ two; because three thirds make a whole one.

EXAMPLES.

(1.)

	$	*cts.*
	5	11
	1	10
	2	50
	8	44
Ans.	17	15

(2.)

	$	*cts.*
	10	30
	5	14
	2	62
	1	75
Ans.	19	81

(3.)

	$	*cts.*
	110	50
	12	25
	9	20
	112	18
Ans.	244	13

(4.)

	$	*cts.*
	125	50
	812	30
	560	12
	12	10
	6	00
	330	01
Ans.	1846	03

(5.)

	$	*cts.*
	120	$18\frac{3}{4}$
	56	25
	130	$12\frac{1}{2}$
	25	25
	72	$56\frac{1}{4}$
	1	09
Ans.	405	$46\frac{1}{2}$

(6.)

	$	*cts.*
	910	$81\frac{1}{4}$
	16	18
	122	$12\frac{1}{2}$
	90	09
	999	99
	125	$06\frac{1}{4}$
Ans.	2263	76

(7.)

	$	*cts.*
	500	00
	200	00
	150	00
	140	00
	130	00
	120	$62\frac{1}{2}$
Ans.	1240	$62\frac{1}{2}$

(8.)

	$	*cts.*
	24	$68\frac{3}{4}$
	19	$37\frac{1}{2}$
	22	50
	17	55
	10	$37\frac{1}{2}$
	1	$06\frac{1}{4}$
	2	$12\frac{1}{2}$
Ans.	97	$67\frac{1}{2}$

(9.)

	$	*cts.*
	40	00
	6	00
	2	00
	2	00
	2	00
	8	75
	1	$12\frac{1}{2}$
	1	$37\frac{1}{2}$
Ans.	58	25

10. Laid out in market for cloth 12 dollars 50 cents; for tobacco 20 dollars 75 cents; for salt 13 dollars 50 cents; for calico 40 dollars; for cinnamon 18 dollars $29\frac{3}{4}$ cents; and for sugar 90 dollars 22 cents. How much did the whole amount to? Ans. 195 dollars $26\frac{3}{4}$ cents.

11. I have bought 4 yards of lace for 5 dollars; a veil for 8 dollars 50 cents; 9 yards of silk for 18 dollars 87½ cents; 12 yards of ribbon for 1 dollar 18¾ cents; 19 yards of linen for 14 dollars 50 cents; 2 pair of gloves for 87½ cents; 3 pieces of domestic for 5 dollars 37½ cents; 9 yards of lace for 7 dollars 87½ cents, and 6 yards of cambrick for 20 dollars. What did the whole amount to?

Ans. 82 dollars 18¾ cents.

12. Bought of Buckner Willingham, cloth for a coat, for 25 dollars; a pair of pantaloons for 12 dollars 50 cents; a vest for 6 dollars 12½ cents; a hat for 8 dollars 50 cents; a shirt for 2 dollars; a cravat for 1 dollar; a pair of socks for 1 dollar 50 cents; a pair of boots for 7 dollars 56¼ cents; a pair of slips for 1 dollar 25 cents; a pair of suspenders for 75 cents; a pair of gloves for 1 dollar; a handkerchief for 1 dollar; and a great coat for 35 dollars. What did the whole suit cost? Ans. 103 dollars 18¾ cents.

13. A gentleman in building a fine house, finds his plank costs 950 dollars; his workmen will have 1000 dollars; the stone will cost 260 dollars; the window glass 40 dollars, boarding his hands 600 dollars. What is the cost of the whole? Ans. 2850 dollars.

14. My agent has bought in market a turkey for 1 dollar 87½ cents; a pair of shoes for 1 dollar 68¾ cents; a ham of pork for 43¾ cents; a quarter of venison for 1 dollar 37½ cents; a piece of beef for 93¾ cents; a hog for 56¼ cents; a quart of strawberries for 37½ cents; some lard for 31¼ cents; and a peck of potatoes for 12½ cents. What did the whole amount to? Ans. 7 dollars 68¾ cents.

15. A man desirous to set up a store, laid out monies as follows, viz: for cloth 650 dollars 91 cents; for iron 220 dollars; for calicoes, &c., 1200 dollars 5 cents; sugar 90 dollars 40½ cents; coffee 559 dollars 99¾ cents; nails 80 dollars; books 1000 dollars; ink-stands 40 dollars; slates 60 dollars; leather 100 dollars; tobacco 96 dollars; blankets 205 dollars 1 cent; cinnamon 13 dollars 51 cents; oil 29 dollars 19 cents; steel 30 dollars 33¼ cents; molasses 16 dollars; hats 109 dollars 4½ cents; castings 400 dollars 55 cents; thread 75 dollars 71¼ cents; and for rum 227 dollars 37½ cents. What is the cost of the whole?

Ans. 5204 dollars 8¾ cents.

AVOIRDUPOIS WEIGHT.

(16.)	T.	cwt.	qr.	lb.		(17.)	T.	cwt.	qr.	lb.	oz.
	2	14	1	5			3	2	1	5	6
	4	11	3	7			4	12	3	7	8
	5	6	2	19			5	6	2	0	2
	1	3	1	6			4	19	0	27	15

Ans. 13 16 0 9   Ans. 18 0 3 12 15

18. Add 12t. 16cwt. 1qr. 19lb. 15oz. 114t. 10cwt. 2qr. 27lb. 4oz. 13dr. 72t. 4cwt. 2qr. 24lb. 14oz. 8dr. 176t. 15cwt. 3qr. 4lb. 15oz. 11dr.   Ans. 376t. 7cwt. 2qr. 21lb. 1oz. 11dr.

19. Add 139t. 19cwt. 3qr. 18lb. 13oz. 10dr. 1754t. 10cwt. 2qr. 11lb. 2oz. 14dr. 27t. 3cwt. 14lb. 11oz. 13cwt. 18oz.
Ans. 1922t. 6cwt. 2qr. 17lb. 8oz. 8dr.

20. Add 20t. 2cwt. 2qr. 12t. 15t. 2qr. and 2t.
Ans. 49t. 3cwt.

TROY WEIGHT.

	lb.	oz.	dwt.			lb.	oz.	dwt.	gr.
(21.)	4	5	6		(22.)	185	2	19	20
	8	9	13			56	9	15	6
	1	4	7			1472	11	2	17
	5	8	11			385	0	8	5
	1	3	2			10	8	7	12
	21	6	19			2110	8	13	12

23. Add 7lb. 9oz. 11dwt. 22gr. 16lb. 4oz. 18dwt. 6gr. 163lb. 7oz. 12dwt. 18gr. 17lb. 13dwt.
Ans. 204lb. 10oz. 15dwt. 22gr.

24. Add 10lb. 5oz. 2dwt. 10gr. 5lb. 10oz. 10dwt. 2gr. 22lb. 9oz. 15dwt. 1gr. 8oz. 10gr. 3lb. 4oz. 2dwt. 1gr.
Ans. 43lb. 1oz. 10dwt.

25. Add 12lb. 10oz. 2dwt. 3gr. 4lb. 5oz. 8dwt. 19gr. 13lb. 7oz. 11dwt.   Ans. 30lb. 11oz. 1dwt. 22gr.

APOTHECARIES' WEIGHT.

(26.)	℔	℥	ʒ	℈	(27.)	℔	℥	ʒ	℈	(28.)	℔	℥	ʒ	℈	gr.
	6	3	2	1		3	2	1	3		10	9	4	2	6
	12	8	1	7		6	4	3	2		19	1	6	4	4
	112	6	3	5		10	0	2	4		7	5	2	3	2
	40	4	1	0		108	6	1	0		126	8	1	1	3
	2	6	2	1		19	4	3	2		1122	2	3	8	1
	174	4	5	2		147	5	5	2		1286	3	6	0	16

29. Add 16lb. 1oz. 1dr. 2sc. 12gr. 175lb. 10oz. 5dr. 10gr.
320lb. 3oz. 1dr. 15gr. 11oz. 2dr. 3sc.

Ans. 513lb. 2oz. 3dr. 0sc. 17gr.

30. Add 18lb. 11oz. 7dr. 1sc. 19gr. 126lb. 7oz. 5dr. 2sc.
15gr. 96lb. 1dr. 3gr.

Ans. 241lb. 7oz. 6dr. 1sc. 17gr.

LONG MEASURE.

(31.)	L.	M.	fur.	P.	(32.)	yd.	ft.	in.
	2	4	7	10		2	1	4
	4	6	5	1		5	2	7
	1	3	2	20		6	0	11
	75	9	8	25		9	3	5
	256	0	1	16		1	1	1
Ans.	346	1	0	32		26	0	4

33. Add 500L. 1M. 2fur. 20P. 1yd. 2ft. 4in. 14P. 1yd.
3in. 1M. 2fur. 29P. 10in. 4fur. 2fur. 10in. 1yd. 2ft. 3in.

Ans. 501L. 0M. 3fur. 23P. 5yd. 0ft. 6in.

34. Add 462L. 1M. 7fur. 29P. 1yd. 1ft. 10in. 11P. 1ft.
10½. 4L. 1M. 2fur. 28P. 1yd. 2ft. 9in. 13P.

Ans. 467L. 3fur. 1P. 4yd. 5in.

CLOTH MEASURE.

(35.)	yd.	qr.	na.	(36.)	yd.	qr.	na.	(37.)	E.E.	qr.	na.
	2	3	4		1	1	1		19	3	2
	5	1	3		2	2	2		4	2	3
	76	2	1		3	3	3		27	3	1
	21	1	2		5	4	2		14	1	4
	106	1	2		14	0	0		66	1	2

38. Add 19yd. 2qr. 3na. 14yd. 2qr. 32yd. 2na. 3qr. 1na.
142yd. 3qr. 2na.

Ans. 210yds.

39. Add 20E.F. 2qr. 3na. 401E.F. 3qr. 2na. 126E.F.
5qr. 1na. 782E.F.

Ans. 1330E.F. 5qr. 2na.

40. Add 2E.Fl. 1qr. 3na. 1E.Fl. 1qr. 1na. 3qr.

Ans. 5E.Fl.

LAND OR SQUARE MEASURE.

(41.)	A.	R.	P.	(42.)	A.	R.	P.	(43.)	A.	R.
	21	0	27		39	2	37		51	0
	19	2	12		62	1	17		17	3
	80	3	13		68	0	38		13	3
	110	1	29		129	3	12		21	1
	224	2	10		532	1	18		1	1
Ans.	456	2	11		832	2	2		105	0

44. Add 620A. 2R. 20P. 908A. 1R. 39P. 173A. 3R. 27P. 1000A. 1R. 17P.   Ans. 2703A. 1R. 23P.

45. Add 999A. 3R. 33P. 1821A. 14P. 25A. 3R. 19P. 150A. 2R. 11P. and 2000A.   Ans. 4997A. 1R. 37P.

LIQUID MEASURE.

(46.)	T.	hhd.	gal.	(47.)	hhd.	gal.	qt.	pt.	gi.
	4	1	3		2	19	0	0	1
	45	3	49		0	0	1	1	0
	75	1	2		3	17	2	0	2
	91	2	58		0	21	0	1	0
	87	3	5		0	0	0	0	1
	304	3	54		5	58	0	1	0

48. Add 24bar. 1gal. 1qt. 1pt. 1gi. 18gal. 2qt. 0pt. 3gi. 1bar. 2gal. 3qt. 2pt. 0gi. 1gal. 2qt. 1pt. 0gi. 6bar.   Ans. 31bar. 19gal. 2qt. 1pt. 0gi.

49. Add 385hhd. 42gal. 3qt. 1pt. 27hhd. 36gal. 2qt. 132hhd. 17gal. 163hhd. 47gal. 2qt. 1pt. 2gi.   Ans. 709hhd. 18gal. 0qt. 0pt. 2gi.

DRY MEASURE.

(50.)	bu.	pe.	qt.	(51.)	bu.	pe.	qt.	pt.	(52.)	bu.	pe.	qt.	pt.
	37	2	1		50	2	7	1		85	1	5	1
	132	3	2		65	3	5	2		96	3	4	0
	423	1	0		185	1	2	0		191	2	3	1
	162	3	1		173	2	1	1		201	1	7	0
	357	0	2		90	3	4	0		909	3	5	1
	1163	1	6		566	1	5	0		1485	1	1	1

53. Add 144bu. 3pe. 2qt. 1pt. 1pe. 2qt. 3qt. 1pt. 462bu. 3pe. 1pt. 72bu. 5qt. 1pt.   Ans. 680bu. 0pe. 6qt. 0pt.

54. Add 60bu. 1pe. 1qt. 1pt. 41bu. 3pe. 4qt. 0pt. 500bu. 2pe. 7qt. 1pt. 183bu. 0pe. 5qt. 0pt.

Ans. 786bu. 0pe. 2qt. 0pt.

TIME.

(55.) Y.	M.	(56.) w.	da.	hr.	min.	(57.) da.	hr.	min.	sec.
80	5	3	2	9	20	4	23	45	30
12	3	1	5	10	30	1	12	14	16
15	7	2	1	9	25	3	19	17	22
20	8	3	3	15	57	2	00	00	10
Ans. 128	11	10	5	21	12	12	7	17	18

58. Add 25y 7m. 12y. 3m. 96y. 10m. 26y. 9m. 11y. 7m. and 9y.

Ans. 182y. 0m.

APPLICATION.

59. Bought potatoes to the amount of $37 50 cts.; corn to the amount of $19 21¼ cts.; wheat to the amount of $81 37½ cts. What is the cost of the whole?

Ans. $138 08¾ cents.

60. Bought pepper to the amount of $358 75 cents; oil to the amount of $105 06¼ cents; molasses to the amount of $4 43¾ cts. What did the whole amount to?

Ans. $468 25 cents.

61. Bought 6 pieces of linen; the first contains 57yds. 2qr.; the second 29yds. 3qr. 2na.; the third 45yds. 1qr.; the fourth 32yds. 3qr. 1na.; and the other two each 38yds. 2qr. What number of yards are there in the whole?

Ans. 242yds. 1qr. 3na.

62. There are 4 bags of corn; the first contains 2bu. 2pe.; the second 3bu. 3pe. 5qt.; the third 3bu. 1pe. 1qt.; the fourth 2bu. and 4qt. How much is in the four bags?

Ans. 11bu. 3pe. 2qt.

63. A man has three farms; the first contains 142a. 2r.; the second 32a. 3r. 12p.; the third 108a. 3r. 18p. How many acres are there in all? Ans. 284a. 0r. 30p.

64. There are 3 pieces of tape; the first measures 15yds. 3qr.; the second 18yds. 1qr. 2na.; the third 25yds. 3qr. 2na. How many yards are there in the three pieces? Ans. 60yds.

65. If a man on a journey, travel the first day 43m. 3fur., the second 29m. 34p., the third 57m. 2fur. 32p., and the fourth 12m. 3fur. 18p., how many miles did he travel in the four days? Ans. 142m. 2fur. 4p.

66. Suppose a man to have, in one barrel 40bu. 3pe. 1qt. of wheat, in another 50bu. 6qt. 1pt., in another 41bu. 2pe., in another 64bu. 5qt., in another 6bu. 1pe., in another 19bu. 1pe. 2qt. 1pt., and in another 65bu. 6qt. 2pt., how many bushels are there in the whole?

Ans. 287bu. 1pe. 6qt. 0pt.

67. Suppose a man has in one trunk 487lb. 10oz. 18dwt. 22gr., in another 500lb. 8oz. 11dwt. 10gr., in another 234lb. 11oz. 10dwt. 16gr., how much has he in all?

Ans. 1223lb. 7oz. 1dwt. 0gr.

68. A physician received from Baltimore three boxes of medicine, which cost him as follows, viz.; the first box $21 32¼ cts.; the second $19 37½ cts.; the third $40 17¾ cts. What did the whole cost? Ans. $80 87½ cts.

COMPOUND MULTIPLICATION.

When the multiplier does not exceed 12, work by

RULE I.

Set down the number to be multiplied, and place the multiplier under its right hand denomination; and in multiplying observe the same rules for carrying from one denomination to another, as in Compound Addition.

Note. If there be ¼ in the sum, divide the multiplier by 4; a ½ by 2; ¾ by 2 and 4; a ⅓ by 3; or if there be a fraction in the multiplier, divide the sum in like manner, and add their amount to the sum produced by the whole number.

EXAMPLES.

FEDERAL MONEY.

	$	*cts.*		$	*cts.*		$	*cts.*
(1.)	2	50	(2.)	12	56¼	(3.)	22	12½
		2			4			6
Ans.	5	00	Ans.	50	25	Ans.	132	75

	$	*cts.*		$	*cts.*		$	*cts.*
(4.)	26	18¾	(5.)	58	78¾	(6.)	125	06¼
		3			5			7
Ans.	78	56¼	Ans.	293	93¾	Ans.	875	43¾

		$	cts.				$	cts.
7.	Multiply	58	06½	by	4	Answer	232	26
8.		25	37½		8		203	00
9.		565	62½		12		6787	50
10.		112	10½		10		1121	05
11.		222	22½		11		2444	47½

AVOIRDUPOIS WEIGHT.

(12.) T.	cwt.	qr.	lb.	(13.) T.	cwt.	qr.	lb.	oz.	dr.	(14.) qr.	lb.	oz.	dr.
8	6	1	16	6	14	2	7	5	2	3	14	6	4
			3						4				8
Ans. 24	19	0	20	26	18	1	1	4	8	28	3	2	0

15. Bought eight bags of sugar, each weighing 2cwt. 1q. 4lb. What is the weight of the whole?

Ans. 18cwt. 1qr. 4lb.

16. Multiply 4cwt. 3qr. 17lb. by 11.

Ans. 53cwt. 3qr. 19lb.

TROY WEIGHT.

(17.) lb.	oz.	dwt.	(18.) lb.	oz.	dwt.	gr.	(19.) lb.	oz.	dwt.	gr.
56	4	14	47	2	0	8	112	8	2	20
		2				3				5
112	9	8	141	6	1	0	563	4	14	4

20. Multiply 96lb. 9oz. 11dwt. 10gr. by 8.

Ans. 774lb. 4oz. 11dwt. 8gr.

APOTHECARIES' WEIGHT.

(21.) ℔	℥	ʒ	℈	(22.) ℔	℥	ʒ	℈	gr.	(23.) ℔	℥	ʒ	℈	gr.
4	8	2	1	47	2	1	2	12	12	3	4	2	0
			5					7					12
Ans. 23	5	3	2	330	3	5	0	4	147	7	0	0	0

24. Multiply 67lb. 6oz. 3dr. 2sc. by 7.

Ans. 472lb. 9oz. 1dr. 2sc.

25. There are 9 parcels, each weighing 109lb. 7oz. 6dr. 2sc. 2gr. what is their weight?

Ans. 986lb. 10oz. 4dr. 0sc. 18gr.

LONG MEASURE.

(26.)	M.	Fur.	P.		(27.)	L.	M.	Fur.	P.
	1	3	36			3	2	1	28
			12						7
	17	6	32			26	0	3	36

28. Multiply 14M. 5Fur. 39P. by 11.
                Ans. 162M. 1 Fur. 29P.

29. Multiply 1L. 2M. 3Fur. 1P. 1yd. 1ft. 2in. by 2.
            Ans. 3L. 1M. 6Fur. 2P. 2yd. 2ft. 4in.

CLOTH MEASURE.

(30.)	yd.	qr.	na.	(31.)	E.E.	qr.	na.	(32.)	E.F.	qr.	na.
	12	3	2		22	2	3		16	2	1
			4				6				8
Ans.	51	2	0		135	1	2		131	0	0

33. If 20yd. 2qr. 3na., be multiplied by 7, what number of yards will there be?   Ans. 144yd. 3qr. 1na.

LAND OR SQUARE MEASURE.

(34.)	A.	R.	P.	(35.)	A.	R.	P.	(36.)	A.	R.	P.
	38	3	13		47	2	10		20	3	30
			2				5				9
	77	2	26		237	3	10		188	1	30

37. Multiply 40A. 1R. 19P. by 12. Ans. 484A. 1R. 28P.

38. How many acres will 7 teams plough in one day, allowing them 1A. 3R. 39P. each? Ans. 13A. 3R. 33P.

LIQUID MEASURE.

(39.)	hhds.	gal.	qt.	(40.)	T.	hhd.	gal.	qt.	pt	(41.)	hhd.	gal.	qt.	pt
	2	13	3		2	1	12	2	1		6	43	2	1
			4						8					7
	8	55	0		18	1	38	0	0		46	53	1	1

42. Multiply 2T. 1p. 40gal. 3qt. 1pt. by 6.
              Ans. 15T. 1p. 1hhd. 56gal. 2qt.

43. Multiply 4T. 1hhd. 10gal. 1pt. by 10.
              Ans. 42T. 3hhd. 38gal. 1qt.

DRY MEASURE.

(44.)	bu.	pe.	qt.	pt.
	180	5	2	1
				8
	1450	2	4	0

(45.)	bu.	pe.	qt.	pt
	12	2	7	1
				3
	38	0	6	1

46. Multiply 120bu. 3pe. 0qt. 2pt. by 4.

Ans. 483bu. 0pe. 4qt. 0pt.

47. Multiply 189bu. 3pe. 7qt. by 7.

Ans. 1329bu. 3pe. 1qt.

48. Multiply 98bu. 0pe. 5qt. 1pt. by 9.

Ans. 883bu. 2pe. 1qt. 1pt.

TIME.

(49.)	Y.	M.
	3	11
		3
	11	9

(50.)	Y.	M.
	8	4
		6
	50	0

(51.)	Y.	W.	D.
	12	19	5
			2
	24	39	3

52. Multiply 49Y. 9M. by 7. Ans. 348Y. 3M.

53. Multiply 19Y. 29Da. by 9. Ans. 171Y. 261Da.

When the multiplier is more than twelve, and is the exact product of two factors in the multiplication table, work by rule 2. Multiply the given sum by one of the factors; then multiply that product by the other factor.

EXAMPLES.

(54.) Multiply	$	cts.	m.		(55.)	$	cts.	
	66	37	5 by 36		5	09 by)		
			6			2		
	398	25	0		10	18		
			6			8		
Ans.	2389	50	0		81	44		

	$	cts.	m.			$	cts.	m
57.	66	37½		by 36	Ans.	2389	50	0
58.	44	25	3	56		2478	16	8
59.	12	18¾		96		1170	00	0
60.	22	12	5	42		929	25	0
61.	26	18	7	48		1256	97	6
62.	75	24	9	81		6095	16	9

	$	cts.				$	cts.	m.
63.	20	08½		by 1·08	Ans.	2169	00	¼ 0
64.	10	12½		144		1458	00	0

	A.	R.	P.			A.	R.	P.
65.	47	3	20	by 54		2585	1	
66.	25	2	. 8	30		766	2	00

	M.	F.	P.			M.	F.	P.
67.	48	7	25	by 88		·4307	7	0

	lb	3	3			lb	3	3
68.	56	9	6	by 84		4772	3	0

When the multiplier is not the exact product of any two factors in the multiplication table, work by rule 3. Use the two factors whose product comes nearest the multiplier; then multiply the given sum by the number which supplies the deficiency, and add its product to the sum produced by the two factors.

EXAMPLES.

		$	cts.	m.
69.	Multiply	2	25	4 × 2* by 52
				10
		22	54	0
				5
		112	70	0
		4	50	8
		117	20	8

*Ten times 5 make 50, and 2 supplies the deficiency.

		$	cts.	m.			$	cts.	m.
70.	Multiply	4	75	8 by 29	Ans.		137	98	2
71.		7	87½	47			370	12½	
72.		28	68¾	68			1950	75	
73.		49	75	87			4328	25	
74.		94	18¾	31			2919	81¼	
75.		42	31¼	58			2454	12½	

76. 7cwt. 3qr. 22lb. by 51.   Ans. 405cwt. 1qr. 2lb.

77. 12lb. 5oz. 8dwt. by 39.   Ans. 485lb. 6oz. 12dwt.

78. 4m.   6fur. 21p. by 87 Ans. 418m.   7fur. 27p.
79. 50a.   2r.   5p.   34   1718a.   0r.   10p.
80. 60bu. 2pe.   5qt.   43   2608bu. 0pe.. 7qt.
81. 2hhd. 4½gal. 2q. 1pt. 17   45hhd. 14gal. 2qt. 1pt.

When the multiplier is greater than the product of any two factors in the multiplication table, work by rule 4.

Multiply continually by as many tens, less one, as there are figures in the multiplier. Then multiply the product of the last ten by the left hand figure of the multiplier. If greater than 1, again multiply the given sum by the units figure of the multiplier; the product of the first ten by the tens figure; the product of the second ten, if any, by the hundreds figure, &c. Then add the products of these several figures together for the answer.

	$ cts.			$ cts. m.
(83.) Multiply 2	02½ × 2 by 222.	(83.) 1	11 2 × 1 by 511.
	10		10

20	25 × 2	11 12	0 × 1
	10		10

202 50		111 20 0	
	2 left hand figure.		5

405 00		556 00 0
4 05		1 11 2
40 50		11 12 0

449 55		568 23 2

		$ cts.			$ cts.
84.	Multiply	5 18¾	by 325	Answer	1685 93¾
85.		1 56½	456		713 64
86.		2 87½	576		1656 00
87.		4 31¼	679		2928 18¾
88.		18 93¾	457		8654 43¾
89.		25 48¼	879		22359 56¼

		yd. ft. in.			yd. ft. in.
90.		5 1 2	504		2716 0 0

		M. Fur. P.			M. Fur. P.
91.		25 3 18	1265		32170 4 10

4

　　　　　　　yd. qr. na.　　　　　　　　　yd. qr. na.
92. Multiply 22 2 1 by 3204.　Ans. 72290 1 0.

APPLICATION.

93. Sold 125 bushels of wheat at 22 cents per bushel.
What did it amount to?　　　　　　　Ans. $27 50 cents.

94. Sold 60 bushels of apples at 15 cents per bushel.
What did they amount to?　　　　　　　　　Ans. $9.

95. If I buy 13 yards of cloth at 10 cents per yard, what
must I pay?　　　　　　　　　　Ans. $1 30 cents.

96. When one cord of wood cost $2 10 cents, what will
be the price of nine cords at the same rate?

　　　　　　　　　　　　　Ans. $18 90 cents.

97. Sold 5 cwt of tobacco at $12 50 cents per cwt., what
did the whole amount to?　　　　Ans. $62 50 cents.

EXAMPLES.

　　　　　$ cts.　　　　　　　　　　$ cts.
(98.) Multiply 10 62½ by 4　(99.) Multiply 5 12½ by 8
　　　　　　4　　　　　　　　　　　　　8
　　　　　———　　　　　　　　　　———
　　　　42 48　　　　　　　　　　40 96
　　　　　　2　　　　　　　　　　　　2
　　　　———　　　　　　　　　　———
Ans. 42 50　　　　　　　　　　40 98

100. Bought 24 bushels of wheat at $1 12½ cents per
bushel. What did the whole amount to?　Ans. $27.

101. Bought 44 bu. of corn at 37½ cents per bushel.
What did the whole cost?　　　　Ans. $16 50 cents.

102. A merchant bought two pieces of linen, the one contained 38 yards and the other 26 yards. What did the two
pieces cost at $3 87½ cents per yard?　　Ans. 248.

103. What cost a box of sugar weighing 106 lbs., at 15½
cents per pound?　　　　　　　　Ans. 16 16½ cts.

104. What will 13½ gallons of molasses come to at 40
cents per gallon?　　　　　　　　Ans. $5 40.

105. How much will 25 bushels of oats come to at 15
cents per bushel?　　　　　　　Ans. $3 75 cents.

COMPOUND SUBTRACTION.

RULE.

Place the numbers under each other which are of the
same denomination: the less always being under the greater.

Begin at the right hand figure, and if it be larger than the one above it, consider the upper one as having as many added to it as make one of the next greater denomination. Subtract the lower from the upper figure thus increased, and set down the remainder, observing to carry one to be added to the next higher denomination, and so proceed.

Proof as in Simple Subtraction.

EXAMPLES.

FEDERAL MONEY.

	$	cts.	m.		$	cts.	m.		$	cts.	m.
(1.)	5	54	7	(2.)	1	50	2	(3.)	19	84	4
	2	10	5			28	4		10	18	9
Ans.	3	44	2		1	21	8		9	65	5

	$	cts.		$	cts.		$	cts.
(4.)	64	87½	(5.)	10	37½	(6.)	100	00
	25	12½		5	06¼			55	62½
	39	75		5	81¼		44	37½

	$	cts.		$	cts.		$	cts.
(7.)	45	64¾	(8.)	30	30	(9.)	150	93¾
	5	99½		1	12½		90	10
	39	65¼		29	17½		60	83¾

10. I owed $559 22¼ cents, but have paid $148 50 cts. How much remains unpaid? Ans. $410 72¼ cents.

11. Lent a man $400; he now returns $211 12½ cents. How much does he still owe? Ans. $188 87½ cents.

12. A merchant had in his desk $500 87½ cents, but drew out $120 93 cts. to pay a debt. How much had he left in the desk? Ans. 379 dollars 94½ cents.

13. I had 303 dollars 6¼ cents, but lent 9 dollars 91¼ cents. How much had I left? Ans. 293 dollars 15 cents.

14. From $1000 take 1 mill. Ans. $999 99 cts. 9m.

AVOIRDUPOIS WEIGHT.

	cwt.	qr.	lb.		T.	cwt.	qr.	lb.
(15.)	6	3	25	(16.)	28	3	1	27
	4	2	12		13	1	0	19
Ans.	2	1	13		15	2	1	08

17. From 14t. 10cwt. 2qr. 16lb. take 11lb.

　　　　　　　　　　　Ans. 14t. 10cwt. 2qr. 5lb.

18. Bought 400cwt. of sugar, but have since sold 2cwt. 3qr. 14lb. What quantity remains?

　　　　　　　　　　　Ans. 397cwt. 0qr. 14lb.

TROY WEIGHT.

	lb.	oz.	dwt.	gr.		lb.	oz.	dwt.	gr.
(19.)	24	6	19	13	(20.)	13	9	5	22
	19	5	18	23		8	11	16	10
Ans.	5	1	0	14		4	9	9	12

21. From 27lb. 9oz. 16dwt. take 19dwt.

　　　　　　　　　　　Ans. 27lb. 8oz. 17dwt.

22. Subtract 1lb. 0oz. 17dwt. 15gr. from 15lb. 9oz. 18dwt. 8gr.　　　　　Ans. 14lb. 9oz. 0dwt. 17gr.

APOTHECARIES' WEIGHT.

	℔	ʒ	ℨ			℔	ʒ	ℨ	℈			℔	ʒ	ℨ	℈
(23.)	186	7	5		(24.)	96	4	0	2		(25.)	100	9	8	2
	67	8	4			75	4	2	1			99	8	3	2
Ans.	118	11	1			20	11	6	1			1	1	5	0

CLOTH MEASURE.

	yds.	qr.	na.		yds.	qr.	na.		yds.	qr.	na.
(26.)	160	3	3	(27.)	969	2	1	(28.)	14	0	3
	37	1	2		786	1	2		9	3	2
Ans.	123	2	1		183	0	3		4	1	1

29. Bought 27 yards of domestic, but have since sold 9yds. 3qr. How much remains?　　　Ans. 17yds. 1qr.

	E.E.	qr.	na.		E.Fr.	qr.	na.		E.Fr.	qr.	na.
(30.)	44	3	2	(31.)	62	2	3	(32.)	27	5	2
	23	3	1		43	3	2		19	3	3
Ans.	21	0	1		18	5	1		8	1	3

LONG MEASURE.

L. M. fur. p. yd. in. ft.							L. M. fur. p. yd. ft. in.						
(33.) 6	2	5	9	4	2	6	(34.) 9	1	7	18	5	1	11
4	3	2	8	1	3	7	7	2	5	19	1	2	9
Ans. 1	2	3	1	2	1	11	1	2	1	39	3	2	2

35. Two men travelling the same road; one travels at the rate of 27m. 2fur. 39p.; the other at the rate of 19m. 1fur. 17p. At night how far are they distant?
Ans. 8m. 1fur. 22p.

LAND OR SQUARE MEASURE.

A. R. P.		A. R. P.		A. R. P.		A. R. P.	
(36.) 96 2 16		(37.) 640 3 12		(38.) 96 0 18		(39.) 50 3 19	
87 3 18		114 4 3		74 2 4		13 1 5	
Ans. 8 2 38		525 3 9		21 2 14		37 2 14	

40. A father dying left his son Joseph 200a. 2r. 20p., and to James 180a. 3r. 39p. What is the difference in their shares? Ans. 19a. 2r. 21p.

LIQUID MEASURE.

T. hhd. gal. qt. pt.					T. hhd. gal. qt.			
(41.) 8	2	42	2	1	(42.) 186	3	9	1
3	2	14	3	0	96	2	8	2
Ans. 5	0	27	3	1	90	1	0	3

43. A person bought 4hhd. 25gal. of cider;—he has since sold 2hhd. 15gal. 3qt. 1pt. How much has he remaining? Ans. 2hhd. 9gal. 0qt. 1pt.

44. If 5hhd. 1gal. 1qt. 1pt. of oil be drawn from 6hhd. 2gal. 2qt. 1pt. how much will remain?
Ans. 1hhd. 1gal. 1qt. 0p.

DRY MEASURE.

bu. pe. qt. pt.				bu. pe. qt. pt.				bu. pe. qt. pt.			
(45.) 44	2	1	1	(46.) 80	3	7	1	(47.) 789	0	5	0
32	3	2	1	15	1	1	1	578	3	6	1
Ans. 11	2	7	0	65	2	6	0	210	0	6	1

48. From 719bu. 3pe. 5qt. take 533bu. 2pe. 6qt.
                       Ans. 186bu. 0pe. 7qt.

49. Raised 189bu. 1pe. 7qt. 1pt. of corn; have since sold 167bu. 2pe. 1qt.; what quantity have I remaining?
                       Ans. 21bu. 3pe. 6qt. 1pt.

TIME.

	Y.	M.		Y.	M.		hr.	min.	sec.
(50.)	12	11	(51.)	7	1	(52.)	18	45	59
	7	5		3	10		2	51	28
Ans.	5	6		3	3		15	54	31

53. Subtract 125y. 9m. from 450y. 11m.
                       Ans. 325y. 2m.

54. Take 36da. 14hr. 30min. and 25sec. from 44da. 1hr. 48min. and 58sec.   Ans. 7da. 11hr. 18min. 33sec.

Note. The interval or space of time between two given dates is thus found: Set down the greater date, and under it the less: Begin with the days. If the upper number of days be greater than the lower, subtract the lower from it, and set down the remainder. But if the lower number be greater, add as many days to the upper as make a month of the lower, and subtract the lower therefrom; then carry one to the months of the less date, and subtract as before, and so proceed.

EXAMPLES.

55. Abijah was born on the 15th of November, 1807, and Josiah on the 16th of July, 1811. What is the difference in their ages?

	Y.	M.	de.
	1811	7*	16
	1807	11	15
Ans.	3	8	1

*Note. —July is the seventh month, and November the eleventh.

56. Charles was born on the 18th day of June, 1821. How old will he be on the 13th day of August, 1840?
                       Ans. 19y. 1m. 25da.

57. William was born on the 11th day of August, 1813, and John on the 5th day of July, 1827. How much older is William than John? Ans. 13y. 10m. 25da.

58. A man gave his note on the 10th day of May, 1824, and lifted it on the 8th day of December, 1829. For what time did he pay interest? Ans. 5y. 6m. 29da.

APPLICATION.

59. Bought 2 pair of stockings, at 75 cts. per pair; 16yds. of linen, at 87½ cts. per yard; 28yds. of domestic, at 22 cts. per yard; and 5 pair of gloves, at 31¼ cts. per pair; and to him from whom I bought those articles, I deliver $50 00, out of which he is to take the sum due him. How much change will there be coming to me? Ans. $26 77¼ cts.

60. If I buy 660yds. of muslin for $90 60 cts., and sell the same again for $100 04 cts., how much do I gain by the sale? Ans. $9 44 cts.

60. Bought 50yds. of superfine cloth at $8 75 cents per yard; 30 pounds of coffee, at 22½ cts. per pound; and 44 bushels of salt, at $2 per bushel. What sum must I pay for the whole? Ans. $532 25 cts.

62. I have several tracts of land; one of them contains 690a. 2r, 16p.; another 400a.; and two others, each 63a. 3r. 24p. If I sell 200 acres, what number remains?
Ans. 1018a. 1r. 24p.

63. Bought 400bu. 3pe. of wheat; 160bu. of rye; 150bu. 2pe. of oats. I have since sold 225bu. 1pe. of wheat; 37bu. 2pe. of rye; 78bu. 3pe. of oats. How many bushels of each have I remaining?
Ans. { 175bu. 2pe. wheat,
122bu. 2pe. rye,
71bu. 3pe. oats.

COMPOUND DIVISION.

Compound Division teaches to divide any sum or quantity which consists of several denominations.

RULE.

Begin at the highest denomination, and divide the several denominations of the given sum or quantity one after another, and set their respective quotients underneath. When a remainder occurs, reduce it to the next lower denomination by multiplying it by as many of the next denomination as make one of that denomination from which the remainder is derived, and the next denomination to the product; then divide as before, and so proceed.

Note. If the dividend be not large enough to contain the divisor reduce it till it will be, and proceed as before.

EXAMPLES.

(1.)	(2.)	(3.)
$ cts.	$ cts. m.	$ cts.
2)12 61	3)187 91 4	4)168 99
Ans. 6 30½	Ans. 62 63 8	Ans. 42 24¾

		$	cts.				$	cts.
4.	Divide	366	18¾	by	3	Ans.	122	06¼
5.		496	75		8		62	09¼ +
6.		384	87½		6		64	14½ +
7.		587	68¾		9		65	29¾ +
8.		976	43¾		11		88	76½ +
9.		1979	33⅓		12		164	94⅓ +

		yd.	qr.	na.				yd.	qr.	na.
10.	Divide	44	1	2	by	7	Ans.	6	1	1 +
11.		56	3	3		11		5	0	2 +

		M.	fur.	P.				M.	fur.	P.
12.	Divide	105	5	22	by	12	Ans.	8	6	18 +
13.		45	7	18		6		7	5	9 +

		bu.	pe.	qt.				bu.	pe.	qt.	pt.
14.	Divide	48	2	0	by	4	Ans.	12	0	4	0
15.		86	3	7		3		28	3	7	1 +

Note. When the divisor is more than 12, work by Long Division. Divide the highest denomination of the given sum by the divisor, and reduce the remainder, if any, to the next lower denomination, adding to it when reduced the number there is of that denomination in the given sum or quantity. Then divide as before, and so proceed.

EXAMPLES.

<table>
<tr><td>$ cts. m.</td><td>$ cts.</td></tr>
</table>

(16.) Divide 88 45 6 by 19.   (17.) Divide 250 50 by 25.

<table>
<tr><td>$ cts. m.</td><td>$ cts.</td></tr>
</table>

19)88 45 6.   (Ans. 4 65 5.   25)250 50.   (Ans. 10 02.
76   25

124   0 50
114   50

105   00
95

106
95

11 Remainder.

	$	cts.	m.	by		Ans.	$	cts.	m.
18. Divide	98	77	8	by	44	Ans.	2	24	4 +
19.		45	66	5	36		1	26	8 +
20.		77	87	5	96		0	81	1 +
21.		288	68¾	0	108		2	67¼	+
22.		496	37½	0	132		3	76	0 +
23.		47	68	7	45		1	05	9 +
24.		196	75	0	78		2	52	2 +
25.		496	87½	0	97		5	12	2 +
26.		376	81¼	0	123		3	06	3 +

27. A laborer received for thirty days $900. How much did he receive per day?   Ans. $30.

28. If a boy receive $60 for twelve months work, how much is that for one month?   Ans. $5.

29. How many bushels of corn may be bought for $400, at $2 per bushel?   Ans. 200 bushels.

30. When 72 bushels of corn cost $56 25 cents, what is the price of one bushel?   Ans. 78cts. 1m. +

31. Suppose $1875 81¼ cents to be equally divided among 125 men, what will be the share of each man?   Ans. $15 00½ cent. +

32. 89 men agree to equally divide 150gals. 2qts. 1pt. of brandy among them, how much will be the share of each ?
Ans. 1gal. 2qt. 1pt. +48.

REDUCTION DESCENDING.

Reduction Descending teaches to change any sum or quantity to a lower denomination, but retaining the same value.

RULE.

Multiply the highest denomination of the given sum or quantity by as many of the next lower denomination as make one of the higher, adding to the product the number there is of that denomination in the given sum or quantity.

Note. To reduce dollars to cents, annex two ciphers to the dollars.

EXAMPLES.

FEDERAL MONEY.

(1.) Reduce $18 50 cts. to cts.
        100
        ――――
Ans. 1850

(2.) Bring $75 to cts.
        100
        ――――
        7500

3. Bring $100 to cents.   Ans. 10000 cents.
4. Reduce 20 dollars to cents.   Ans. 2000 cents.
5. Bring 25 dollars to cents.   Ans. 2500 cents.
6. Reduce 45 dollars to cents.   Ans. 4500 cents.

Note. To reduce dollars to halves, quarters or thirds of a cent, bring them first into cents, and then bring the cents into halves, quarters or thirds, as required.

(7.) Bring $50 into half cts.
        100
       ――――
       5000
          2
       ――――
Ans. 10000 halves.

(8.) Bring $40 into thirds of a ct.
        100
       ――――
       4000
          3
       ――――
Ans. 12000 thirds.

(9.) Reduce 25 cts. to fourths.
        4
       ――
Ans. 100 fourths.

(10.) Reduce 12 cts. to thirds.
        3
       ――
Ans. 36 thirds.

11. Reduce 10 dollars to dimes.   Ans. 100 dimes.

12. Reduce 220 dollars to mills.   Ans. 220,000 mills.
13. Reduce $426 88½ cts. to halves of a cent.
                                    Ans. 85377 halves.
14. Bring $487 44¾ cents to fourths of a cent.
                                    Ans. 194979 fourths.
15. Bring $17 18¾ cents to fourths of a cent.
                                    Ans. 6875 fourths.

AVOIRDUPOIS WEIGHT.

16. Bring 2 tons to cwt. (17.) Reduce 260 cwt to quarters.
         20   4
         --   ---
    Ans. 40 cwt.   Ans. 1040 quarters.

18. Reduce 36qr. to pounds.   Ans. 1008lb.
19. Bring 17 pounds to ounces.   Ans. 272oz.
20. Bring 2qr. 25lb. 10oz. to drams.   Ans. 20896dr.

TROY WEIGHT.

21. Reduce 20 pennyweights to grains.
             24

             80
             40

    Ans. 480 grains.

22. Reduce 5 ounces to grains.   Ans. 2400gr.
23. Bring 40 pounds to pennyweights.   Ans. 9600dwt.
24. How many grains are there in 19lb. 11oz. 14dwt.
21gr.   Ans. 115077gr.

APOTHECARIES' WEIGHT.

25. Reduce 40 pounds to ounces.   Ans. 480oz.
        12

        480
26. Bring 72oz. to drams.   Ans. 576dr.
27. Reduce 15lb. 9oz. 4dr. 2sc. 17gr. to grains.
                                    Ans. 91017gr.

LONG MEASURE.

28. Reduce 10ft. to inches.   Ans. 120in.
        12

        120

29. Bring 40yd. to feet.   Ans. 120ft.
30. Reduce 120yd. 1ft. 4in. to inches.   Ans. 4336in.
31. Reduce 20 miles to yards.   Ans. 35200yd.
32. Reduce 450m. 6fur. 32p. to poles.   Ans. 144272p.
33. In 2L. 1m. 3fur. 16p. 3yd. 2ft. 10in. how many inches?   Ans. 470590in.

CLOTH MEASURE.

34. Reduce 22 quarters to nails.   Ans. 88na.

        4
        —
       88

35. Bring 36yd. to qr.   Ans. 144qr.
36. Bring 20 English Ells to quarters.   Ans. 100qr.
37. Bring 20 French Ells to quarters.   Ans. 120qr.
38. Bring 8yd. 1qr. to qr.   Ans. 33qr.
39. In 19yd. 2qr. 1na. how many nails? Ans. 313na.

LAND OR SQUARE MEASURE.

40. Bring 2 roods to perches.   Ans. 80 perches.

      40
      —
     80

41. Reduce 140 acres to perches.   Ans. 22400 perches.
42. Bring 54 acres, 3 roods, 23 poles, to poles.
                        Ans. 8783p.
43. Bring 6 square feet to square inches.   Ans. 864in.
44. Bring 120 square yards to square inches.
                     Ans. 155520in.
45. Bring 29 square yards, 2 square feet, 102 square inches to square inches.   Ans. 37974 square inches.

LIQUID MEASURE.

46. Reduce 31 quarts to pints.   Ans. 62pt.

      2
      —
     62

47. Bring 28 gal. to quarts.   Ans. 112qt.
48. Reduce 5hhd. to gallons.   Ans. 315gal.
49. In 6 tons, how many pints?   Ans. 12096pt.
50. Reduce 4hhd. 3qt. to pints.   Ans. 2022pt.
51. Bring 5 tons. 1hhd. 15gal. 1qt. 1pt. to pints.
                       Ans. 10707pt.

DRY MEASURE.

52. Reduce 16qt. to pints.   Ans. 32pts.
2
—
32

53 Bring 32pe. to quarts.   Ans. 256qt.
54. Reduce 7bu tc pecks.   Ans. 28pe.
55. Reduce 12bu. to pints.   Ans. 768pts.
56. Bring 24bu. 1pe. 2qt. 1pt. to pints.   Ans. 1557pt.

TIME.

57. Bring 40 minutes to seconds.   Ans. 2400sec.
60
—
2400

58. Bring 20 hours to seconds.   Ans. 72000sec
59. Reduce 12 years to months.   Ans. 144m.
60. Bring 45 years to days.   Ans. 16425da.
61. Reduce 3 days, 5hr. 29min. to minutes.
Ans. 4649min

62. Reduce 7y. 3w. 4da. 20hr. 20min. and 20sec. to
seconds.   Ans. 222380420sec

REDUCTION ASCENDING.

Reduction Ascending teaches to change any sum or quantity to a higher denomination.

RULE.

Divide the given sum or quantity in the lowest denomination, by as many of that denomination as make one of the next higher, and so on, until you have brought it into that denomination which your question requires.

Note. Mills may be brought to dollars, cents and mills, by cutting off one figure on the right for mills, two more for cents; the rest will be dollars. Or to bring cents to dollars and cents, cut off two figures on the right for cents.

EXAMPLES.
FEDERAL MONEY.

1. Bring 2800 cents to dollars.   Ans. $28.
28|00

2. Bring 11222 mills to dollars, cents and mills.
    11|22|2   Ans. $11 22cts. 2m.

3. Bring 4444 cents to dollars and cents.
                         Ans. $44 44cts.

4. Bring 864 halves of a cent to whole cents.
                         Ans. 432cts.

5. In 963 thirds how many cents?   Ans. 321cts.
6. In 591 fourths how many cents?   Ans. 147¾cts.
7. Bring 630 thirds to cents.   Ans. 210cts.

AVOIRDUPOIS WEIGHT.

8. Bring 118lb. to quarters.
    28)118(Ans. 4qr. 6lb.
       112
       ———
         6

9. Bring 90qr. to cwt.   Ans. 22cwt. 2qr.
10. Bring 1781lb. to cwt.   Ans. 15cwt. 3qr. 17lb.
11. In 1872dr. how many pounds?   Ans. 7lb. 5oz.
12. Bring 75cwt. to tons.   Ans. 3t. 15cwt.
13. Bring 9856lb. to cwt.   Ans. 88cwt.

TROY WEIGHT.

14. Bring 186oz. to pounds.   Ans. 15lb. 6oz.
    12)186
       ———
       15lb. 6oz.

15. In 544dwt. how many pounds?   Ans. 2lb. 3oz. 4dwt.
16. Bring 960dwt. to pounds.   Ans. 4lb.
17. Bring 9624gr. to pounds.   Ans. 1lb. 8oz. 1dwt.

APOTHECARIES' WEIGHT.

18. Bring 2403 to scruples.   Ans. 12℈.
    3|0)24|0
       ———
        12

19. Bring 2720℈ to ounces.   Ans. 11℥3 2℈.
20. Bring 12660gr. to pounds.   Ans. 2℔ 23 3℈.
21. In 155520gr. how many pounds?   Ans. 27℔.

LONG MEASURE.

22. Bring 120 miles to leagues.   Ans. 40.
    3)120
       ———
        40

23. Bring 1280 poles to fur. Ans. 32fur.
24. Bring 2880 poles to leagues. Ans. 31.
25. Bring 5760 poles to leagues. Ans. 61.

CLOTH MEASURE.

26. In 60 quarters how many yards? Ans. 15yds.

4)60

15

27. Bring 4000 nails to yards. Ans. 250yds.
28. Bring 1260 quarters to E. F. Ans. 210 E. F.
29. Bring 1818 nails to yards. Ans. 113yds. 2qr. 2na.

LAND OR SQUARE MEASURE.

30. In 2400 perches how many Roods? Ans. 60 R.

4|0)240|0

60

31. Bring 2040 perches to Acres. Ans. 12A. 3R.
32. Bring 1908020 perches to A. Ans. 11925A. 0R. 20P.
33. In 1728 square inches how many square feet?
Ans. 12 feet.

LIQUID MEASURE.

34. In 480 gills how many pints? Ans. 120 pts.

4)480

120

35. Bring 1840 pts. to gals. Ans. 230 gals.
36. Bring 1890 gal. to hhds. Ans. 30 hhds.
37. In 504 gallons how many bar.? Ans. 16 bar.

DRY MEASURE.

38. In 800 pints how many qts.? Ans. 400 qts.

2)800

400

39. Bring 240 pints to pe. Ans. 15 pe.
40. Bring 8888 pecks to bu. Ans. 2222 bu.
41. In 12840 pints how many bu.? Ans. 200bu. 2pe. 4qt.

TIME.

42. Bring 2400 seconds to minutes.   Ans. 40 min.

6|0)240|0
———
40

43. In 7200 seconds how many hours?   Ans. 2 hours.
44. Bring 144 months to years.   Ans. 12 years.
45. In 4649 minutes how many days?

Ans. 3da. 5hr. 29m.

PROMISCUOUS EXAMPLES.

1. In 20 dollars how many cents?   Ans. 2000 cents.
2. In 63 roods how many perches?   Ans. 2520 per.
3. How many miles are there in 98 fur.? Ans. 12m. 2fur.
4. In 175 pecks how many bushels?   Ans. 43bu. 3pe.
5. How many min. are there in 720 sec.? Ans. 12min.
6. In 103 pints how many quarts?   Ans. 51qts. 1pt.
7. In 1824 cents how many dollars?   Ans. $18 24 cts.
8. In 8t. 15cwt. how many hundred weight?

Ans. 175 cwt.

9. How many English Ells are there in one hundred
   quarters of a yard?   Ans. 20 E. Ells.
10. How many scruples are there in 9 ℨ?   Ans. 27 ℈.
11. In 203 days how many weeks?   Ans. 29w.
12. In 108dwt. how many ounces?   Ans. 5oz. 8dwt.
13. How many cwt. are there in 20 tons? Ans. 400cwt.
14. In 202 cents how many qrs. of a cent? Ans. 808qrs.
15. How many dollars are there in 8762 cents?

Ans. $87 62cts.

16. How many fur. are there in 3m. 1fur.? Ans. 25fur.
17. In 13lb. avoirdupois how many drams? Ans. 3328dr.
18. In 21 gallons 3qts. 1pt. how many pints?

Ans. 175 pints.

19. How many Ells F. are there in 60 qrs.? Ans. 10E.F.
20. How many lbs. are there in 2461 dwt.

Ans. 10lb. 3oz. 1dwt.

21. How many drams are there in 725lb. 6oz. av.?

Ans. 185696dr.

22. In 12yds. 2qrs. 1na. how many nails? Ans. 201na.
23. How many cwt. are there in 27552lb.? Ans. 246cwt.

RULE OF TWO.

The Rule of Two is that in which two terms are given to find a third, which is the answer.

To find the whole cost of any number of articles at any price per article.

RULE.

Multiply the articles by the given price of one article; the product will be the answer.

EXAMPLES.

1. What will eleven oranges come to at 12½ cents each?

2. How much will 60 bushels of apples come to at 8¼ cents per bushel?

11		60
12½	the given pr. of one article.	8¼
132		480
5½	the half of 11 is 5½	15 the fourth of 60 is 15
Ans. $1 37½		Ans. $4 95

3. How much will 105 pounds of sugar come to at 12½ cts. per pound? Ans. $13 12½ cents.

4. What will 60 apples come to at 2¼ cents each? Ans. $1 35 cents.

5. What will 87½ pounds of beef come to at three cents per pound? Ans. $2 62½ cents.

6. Bought 40 pounds of coffee at 31¼ cents per pound; what did it amount to? Ans. $12 50 cts.

7. Purchased ninety gallons of molasses at 56¼ cents per gallon; what did it amount to? Ans. $50 62½ cts.

8. What will nineteen pounds of bacon come to at 8⅓ cents per pound? Ans. $1 58⅓ cents.

9. What is the cost of 400 pounds of cheese at 8⅓ cents per pound? Ans. $33 33⅓ cents.

10. Bought 101 bushels of wheat at $1 04 cents per bushel; what did it amount to? Ans. $105 04 cents.

11. What will 62½ gallons of whiskey come to at 62½ cents per gallon? Ans. $39 06¼ cents.

12. What will 25 bushels of oats come to at 25 cents per bushel? Ans. $6 25 cents.

13. How much will eleven pounds of butter come to at 8½ cents per pound? Ans. 91¾ cents.

14. What will 84 pounds of lard come to at ten cents per pound? Ans. $8 40 cents.

15. How much will two thousand books come to at 20 cents per book? Ans. $400.

16. What cost 789 pounds of iron at 4½ cents per pound? Ans. $35 50½ cents.

17. What cost 40 bushels of rye, at 20 cts. per bushel? Ans. $8.

18. What will 6 pounds of soap come to at ten cents per pound? Ans. 60 cents.

When it is required to know how many articles may be bought with any sum of money.

RULE.

Divide the sum by the price of one article; have the dividend and divisor of one denomination. The quotient will be the number of articles.

EXAMPLES.

1. How many pounds of butter may be bought with $1 60 cents, at 8 cents per pound?

2. How many pounds of iron can I buy with $7 00 cts. at 3½ cents per pound?

Price of article. 8)1 60

Ans. 20 lbs.

3½ 7 00
2 2

halves. 7) 14 00 halves.

Ans. 200 pounds.

3. When one pound of sugar costs 12½ cents, how many pounds may be had for 30 dollars? Ans. 240 pounds.

4. A gentleman gave his son 60 dollars, which he was to lay out for tea at 37½ cents per pound. How many pounds did he buy? Ans. 160 pounds.

5. How many bushels of corn can I buy for 400 dollars, if I give 13 cents per bushel?

Ans. 3076bu. 3pe. 5qt. 1pt. +

6. When I can buy one pound of tobacco for 25 cents, how many pounds can I buy for $75? Ans. 300 pounds.

7. How many pounds of iron may be bought with 37 dollars, at 4 cents per pound? Ans. 925 pounds.

8. Having $378 10 cents, and wishing to purchase feathers, what quantity can I purchase at 33⅓ cents per pound? Ans. 1134¼ pound. +

9. If sixty dollars be the price of an acre of land, how many acres can I have for $192 60 cents?

Ans. 3a. Or. 33p. +

10. Suppose a man has $1900 06¼ cents, and is desirous to purchase salt. How many bushels can he buy, at 1 dollar 62½ cents? Ans. 1169¼ bu. +

11. How many pounds of coffee, at 22 cents per pound, can I have for 22 dollars? Ans. 100 pounds.

12. How many pounds of pork, at three cents per pound, can I have for 960 dollars 60 cents? Ans. 32020 pounds.

13. How many yards of cloth, at 15 cents per yard, can I have for 450 dollars 45 cts.? Ans. 3003 yards.

14. How many fowls, at 6¼ cents each, can I buy for ninety dollars? Ans. 1440 fowls.

When a number of articles cost any sum of money, and the price of one article is required at the same rate.

RULE.

Divide the whole cost by the number of articles; the quotient will be price of one article.

Note. If the dividend be not large enough to contain the divisor, reduce it till it will be.

EXAMPLES.

1. If 100 bushels of corn cost 12 dollars 50 cents, what is the price of one bushel at the same rate?

2. If 4½ pounds of pepper cost $2 00 cents, what cost one pound at the same rate?

The articles. 10|0 12 5|0   4½ 2 00
                              2   2
         Ans. 12½ cts.   ―――――――――――
                             9) 4 00
                              ――――――――――
                           Ans. 44 cts. 4m. +

3. If 6 fish cost 50 cts., what will one cost?

Ans. 8⅓ cents.

4. If I buy 40 bushels of flaxseed for 40 dollars 40 cents, how much do I give per bushel? Ans. $1 01 cent.

5. A man travelled 420 miles in twelve days. How far did he travel each day? Ans. 35 miles.

6. Bought 120 pair of shoes for 400 dollars 60 cents. What was the cost of one pair? Ans. $3 33⅓ cts.

7 Bought 6000 gallons of whiskey for nine hundred dollars. What was the price of one gallon?

Ans. 15 cents.

8. If I buy 1517½ acres of land for 7500 dollars 37½ cents, how much does it cost me per acre?

Ans. $4 94⅓ cts. +

9. A merchant bought 1950 penknives for 960 dollars 44⅓ cents. What did one cost? Ans. 49⅓ cts. +

10. If I buy 22½ yards of cloth with 7 dollars 50 cents, what cost one yard? Ans. 33⅓ cents.

11. I was offered 2000 books for $500 00 cents. Tell me what one book would cost at that rate? Ans. 25 cents.

12. I was offered 2000 books for $380 50 cents. How much was that for one book? Ans. 19 cents. +

13. When a man's yearly income is $474 50 cents, how much is it per day? Ans. $1 30 cents.

14. If seven months' work bring $25 00 cents, how much will one month bring? Ans. $3 57 cents. +

15. Suppose the President of the United States receive $25000 00 cents a year, how much is that per day?

Ans. $68 49 cts. 3m. +

PROPORTION; OR, RULE OF THREE.

The Rule of Three is that in which three terms are given to find a fourth or answer.

RULE.

Set that term in the third place which is the same kind of the answer. Consider from the nature of the question whether the answer ought to be greater or less than this third term. If it is to be greater, set the greater of the two remaining terms in the middle for the second, and the less for the first; but if it is to be less, set the less of those two terms in the middle for the second term, and the other for the first. Then have the first and second terms of one denomination. If the third term consist of several denominations, reduce it to the lowest denomination in it; then multiply the second and third terms together, and divide the product by the first term. The answer will be of the same denomination as the third term.

Note. The operation may frequently be performed, thus: If the first term will divide the second by the quotient, multiply the third; or if the second will divide the first by the quotient, divide the third term.

EXAMPLES.

1. If four bushels of corn cost 80 cents, how much will 8 bushels cost?

2. If three yards of cloth cost fifty cents, how much will ten yards cost?

bu.	bu.	cts.		yd.	yd.	cts.
4	: 8 :	: 80		3	: 10 :	: 50
		2				10

Ans. $1 60   3 | 500

Ans. $1 66⅔

3. If four yards of muslin cost six cents, what will eight cost?   Ans. 12 cents.

4. If six yards of cloth cost 17 cents, what will seven yards come to at the same rate?   Ans. 19 cents 8m. +

5. If five bushels of potatoes cost 80 cents; what cost 14 bushels at the same rate?   Ans. $2 24 cents.

6. If four bushels of corn cost $2 00 cents, how much will 12 bushels cost at the same rate?   Ans. $6 00 cents.

7. If eight yards of silk cost 40 cents, how much will 16 yards cost?   Ans. 80 cents.

8. If three pounds of cheese cost 10 cents, what will 80 pounds come to at the same rate?   Ans. $2 66⅔ cents.

9. If six pounds of coffee cost 55 cents, what will 75 pounds come to at the same rate?   Ans. $6 87½ cts.

10. If 2¼ bushels of salt cost $4 08 cents, how much will 15¼ bushels come to at the same rate?
Ans. $24 88¼ cents.

11. Bought 24 pounds of beef for \$1 62½ cents, how much is 90½ pounds worth at that rate?
Ans. \$6 12¾ cents. +

12. What are 60 bushels of apples worth, when 13 bushels cost 45 cents? Ans. 2 dollars 07⅔ cents. +

13. If 8 bushels of potatoes cost 3 dollars 94 cents, what will 105 bushels cost? Ans. 51 dollars 71¼ cents.

14. If 45 cents buy 11 pounds of tobacco, how much will 91⅔ cents buy at that rate? Ans. 22⅓lb. +

15. What will 22 books come to, if 60 cost 20 dollars 51 cents? Ans. 7 dollars 52 cents. +

16. If 1 yard 2 quarters of cloth cost 56¼ cents, what will 17 yards 1 quarter cost? Ans. 6 dollars 46¾ cts. +

17. If 4 dollars will pay for 16 days' work, how many days work may be had for 98 dollars? Ans. 392 days.

18. If 2½ bushels of salt cost 2 dollars 62½ cents, how many bushels may be had for 556 dollars 18¾ cents?
Ans. 529⅔ bushels. +

19. If 7 pounds of coffee cost 87½ cents, what must I pay for 244 pounds? Ans. 30 dollars 50 cts.

20. If 450 barrels of flour cost 1350 dollars, what will 8 barrels cost? Ans. 24 dollars.

21. If 750 men require 22500 rations of bread for a month, what will a garrison of 1200 require?
Ans. 36000 rations.

22. If 12 men can do a piece of work in 20 days, in what time will 18 men do it? Ans. 13⅓ days.

23. What will be the cost of 17 tons of lead, if 5 tons cost 500 dollars? Ans. 1700 dollars.

24. If a pasture be sufficient for 3000 horses 18 days, how long will it be sufficient for 2000? Ans. 27 days.

25. If 8 men can build a tower in 12 days, in what time can 12 do it? Ans. 8 days.

26. How much carpeting that is 1½ yards in breadth, will cover a floor that is 7½ yards in length, and 5 yards in breadth? Ans. 25 yards.

27. How many yards of matting, 2½ feet broad, will cover a floor that is 27 feet long and 20 feet broad? Ans. 72yds.

28. What must be the length of a board that is 9 inches in width, to make a surface of 144 inches or a square foot?
Ans. 16 inches.

29. If 5 yards of cloth cost 1 dollar 12½ cents, what is

the value of 4 pieces, each containing 8 yards and 1 quarter? Ans. 7 dollars 42½ cents.

30. If 1½ ounces of spice cost 13 cents, what cost 16½ ounces? Ans. 1 dollar 40¾ cents. +

31. If 100 skeins of silk cost 25 dollars 21 cents, how many may be bought for 1800 dollars 50 cents?
Ans. 7142 skeins. +

32. If 2 dollars 50 cents pay for two weeks' boarding, how long can I board for 40 dollars 40 cents!
Ans. 32 weeks 2 days. +

33. Suppose A hired to B 12 months for 60 dollars, after working 7 months B agreed to pay A at that rate, what must he pay? Ans. 35 dollars.

34. If 1 cwt. of sugar cost 11 dollars 37½ cents, what will 18cwt. 3qr. 19lb. cost? Ans. 215 dollars 21 cts. + 10½

35. How many men will it require to repair a piece of work in 50 days, when 14 men can do it in 100 days?
Ans. 28 men.

36. In what time will 600 dollars gain the interest which 80 dollars would gain in 15 years? Ans. 2 years.

37. If 2 yards of tape cost 50 cents, what will 54 English Ells 3qr. cost at the same rate? Ans. 17 dollars 6¼ cts.

38. If the price of 1 acre of land be 5 dollars 25 cents, what will 350 acres 1 rood 18 perches come to at that rate?
Ans. 1839 dollars 40 cts. 3m. +

Note. In all cases wherein labor is required to be performed, the day must be reckoned at 12 hours.

39. Suppose 20 days be required for 12 men to build a house, in what time can 18 men do the same?
Ans. 13da. 4hr.

40. In what time will 48 men·make a fence which 12 men can do in 24 days? Ans. 6da.

41. If 6 men can do a piece of work in 18 days, how long will it require 12 men to do it? Ans. 9da.

42. If 8 men can mow a piece of meadow in 24 days, how many men can do it in 4 days? Ans. 48 men.

43. If a traveller perform a journey in 5 days, when the days are 11 hours long, how long will he require to do it when the days are 15 hours long? Ans. 3da. 8hr.

44. How many yards of paper 2½ feet wide will be

required to cover a wall which is 12 feet long and 9 feet high?   Ans. 14yd. 1ft. 2in. +

45. What quantity of linen that is 3 quarters of a yard wide, will line 7½ yards of cloth that is 1½ yards wide?
                                                   Ans. 15 yards.

46. A ship's crew consisting of 45 men are provided with 4500 pounds of bread, of which each man eats one pound per day; how many weeks will it last them?
                                                   Ans. 14w. 2da.

PROMISCUOUS EXAMPLES,
IN THE RULE OF TWO AND THREE.

47 If 7 oxen be worth 10 cows, how many cows will 21 oxen be worth?   Ans. 30 cows.

48. If board for one year amount to 182 dollars, what will 39 weeks come to?   Ans. $136 50 cts.

49. If 30 bushels of rye be bought for 120 bushels of potatoes, how many bushels of rye can be bought for 600 bushels of potatoes?   Ans. 150bu. rye.

50. A farmer made 146 barrels of cider, which he afterwards sold at 3 dollars 12½ cents a barrel; what was the amount of the whole?   Ans. 456 dollars 25 cts.

51. A lady purchased a set of silver weighing 5lb. 6oz. 5dwt. at 1 dollar 50 cents an ounce; what was the cost of the whole?   Ans. $90 37½ cts.

52. A lady intending to make a bed-quilt containing 6 square yards, desired her daughter to inform her how much domestic, 3 quarters of a yard wide, would be required to line the same.   How many did it take?   Ans. 8yds.

53. A pipe will drain off a cistern of water in 12 hours. How many pipes of the same size will empty it in 30 minutes?   Ans. 24 pipes.

54. A gentleman bought a bag of coffee for his own use, weighing 127lb., for which he gave 15 dollars 25 cents. What was it a pound?   Ans. 12 cts. +

55. If a man spend 4 dollars 62½ cents each day, how much will that amount to in a year?   Ans. 1688 12½ cts.

56. I lent my friend 350 dollars for five months, he promising to do me the same favor, but when requested, he could spare only 125 dollars.   How long ought I to keep it to balance the favor?   Ans. 14 months.

57 If a person's income be 1000 dollars a year, how

much can he save provided he spend $1 50 cents each day? Ans. 452 dollars 50 cts.

58. If the third of six be three, what may one-fourth of twenty be? As 2 : 5 : : 3. Ans. 7¼.

59. If 30 days tuition cost 3 dollars 50 cents, how much is one day worth at that rate? Ans. 11⅔ cts.

60. How many planks 6 inches wide and 12 feet long will it require to lay a floor that is 18 feet wide and 24 feet long? Ans. 72 planks.

61. A certain boat is 80 feet long and 18 feet wide. I demand the number of planks required to floor it, 13 feet long and 1 foot 3 inches wide? Ans. 88½. +

Note. The diameter of a circle given to find the circumference. State, if 7 give 22, what will the diameter give? Or the circumference given to find the diameter. As 22 is to 7, so is the circumference.

62. If a wheel be 20 feet in diameter, what is its circumference? 7 : 20 : : 22. (Ans. 62⅞.

63. If a wheel be 60 feet in circumference, what is its diameter? 22 : 60 : : 7. (Ans. 19. +

DOUBLE RULE OF THREE.

Double Rule of Three is that in which five terms are given to find the sixth or answer.

RULE.

That which is the principal cause of gain, loss, or action, is the first term. Space of time or distance of place the second. The gain, loss, or the action, the third. Then place the other two terms under those of the same name. If the blank fall under the third term, multiply the first and second terms together for a divisor; the other three for a dividend. But if the blank fall under the first or second terms, multiply the third and fourth terms together for a divisor; the other three for a dividend. The answer will be of the same denomination as the blank term.

Note. If the blank fall under the third term, it is direct proportion. If under the first or second, inverse proportion.

EXAMPLES.

1. If 6 men in 10 days mow 60 acres of grass, how long will it take 5 men to mow 80 acres?

2. If 7 men can reap 84 acres of wheat in 12 days, how many men can reap 100 acres in 5 days?

```
men.  da.   A.              men.  da.   A.
  6 : 10 :: 60               7 : 12 :: 84
  5        80                5        100
 60        10                         12
 ___       ___              ___      ____
300        800              84       1200
             6               5          7
                           ___      ____
    3|00)48|00             42|0) 840|0 (Ans. 20 men.
                                  84
       Ans. 16 days.              __
                                   0
```

3. If 4 men in 8 days eat 5lb. of bread, how much will 12 men eat in 20 days?   Ans. 37½lb.

4. Suppose 4 men mow 48 acres in 12 days, how many acres can 8 men mow in 16 days?   Ans. 128a.

5. If $100 gain $6 in twelve months, what will $400 gain in 9 months?   Ans. 18 dollars.

6. If 8 men in 16 days can earn 96 dollars, how much can 12 men earn in 26 days?   Ans. 234 dollars.

7 If ten men in 18 days can earn 56 dollars, how many dollars can 20 men earn in 35 days?
                                    Ans. $217 77cts. 7m. +

8. Suppose 8 men can make 120 pair of shoes in 30 days, how many can 12 men make in 90 days?   Ans. 540 pair.

9. If 56 dollars 31¼ cents be the wages of 20 men for 5 days, what will 46 men earn in 32 days?   Ans. $828 92cts.

10. If 100 dollars in a year give 6 dollars interest, what will 335 dollars give in 3 years?   Ans. 60 dollars 30 cts.

11. When 10 oxen in 18 days eat 2 acres of grass, how many acres will serve 20 oxen 27 days?   Ans. 6 acres.

12. Suppose the wages of 6 persons for 21 weeks be 288 dollars, what must 14 persons receive for 46 weeks?
                                    Ans. 1472 dollars.

13. If 37lb. of beef be sufficient for 12 persons 4 days, how many pounds will suffice 38 men 16 days?
                                    Ans. 468lb. 10⅔oz.

14. If 30 horses in 4 days eat 40 bushels of corn, how many bushels will suffice 100 horses 20 days?

Ans. 666⅔bu.

15. If the carriage of 9cwt. 45 miles, cost 54 dollars 54 cents, how far may 36cwt. be carried for 98 dollars 72 cts.?

Ans. 20m. 2fur. 36p. +

16. If 100 dollars in 12 months gain 6 dollars interest, what will be the interest of 400 dollars for 14 months?

Ans. 28 dollars.

17. If 100 dollars in 12 months gain 8 dollars interest, what sum will gain 50 dollars in 24 months?

Ans. 312 dollars 50 cts.

18. If 100 dollars in 365 days gain 6 dollars interest, what will be the interest of 1000 dollars for 27 days?

Ans. 4 dollars 44 cts. nearly.

19. If 100 dollars in 52 weeks gain 10 dollars interest, what will be the interest of 75 dollars for 7 weeks?

Ans. 1 dollar 00¾ ct.

20. If 12 bushels of oats be sufficient for 20 horses 22 days, how many bushels will serve 62 horses 36 days?

Ans. 60bu. 3pe. 3qt. 1pt. +

21. When 4 boys, in 20 days, collect 1500 bushels of apples, how many days will it require 25 persons to collect 4000 bushels? Ans. 8 days. +

22. What is the interest of 563 dollars for 4½ years, at 6 per cent. per annum? Ans. 152 dollars 01 ct.

23. What will be the interest of 80 dollars for 10 months at 10 per cent.? Ans. 6 dollars 66⅔ cts.

24. If 100 dollars in 12 months gain 33 dollars 33⅓ cts., what will be the interest of 64 dollars for 8½ months?

Ans. 15 dollars 11 cts. +

25. If 100 dollars in one year gain 7 dollars 50 cents interest, what sum will gain 9 dollars in 4 months?

Ans. 360 dollars.

26. What is the interest of 19 dollars for 5¼ months at 6 per cent.? Ans. 49¾ cts. +

27. What sum at 6 per cent. will produce 500 dollars interest in one year? Ans. 8333⅓ dollars.

28. A gentleman said the money he had on interest at 6 per cent., produced one dollar per day. What sum had he on interest? Ans. 6083⅓ dollars.

29. With how many dollars could I gain 6 dollars in one

year, if with 560 dollars I gain 56 dollars in one year and
8 months?   Ans. 100 dollars.

30. A wall which is to be built to the height of 40 feet
has been raised 20 feet in 10 days by 16 men, how many
men must be employed to finish the work in 5 days?

Ans. 32 men.

PRACTICE.

Practice is a short method of ascertaining the value of
any number of articles at any given price per article.

TABLE OF ALIQUOT PARTS.

cts.	$		qr.	lb.	cwt.
50	= $\frac{1}{2}$			2 or 56	= $\frac{1}{2}$
25	$\frac{1}{4}$		1	28	$\frac{1}{4}$
20	$\frac{1}{5}$			16	$\frac{1}{7}$
12½	$\frac{1}{8}$			14	$\frac{1}{8}$
10	$\frac{1}{10}$			8	$\frac{1}{14}$
8⅓	$\frac{1}{12}$			7	$\frac{1}{16}$
6¼	$\frac{1}{16}$				
5	$\frac{1}{20}$				
4	$\frac{1}{25}$				
2	$\frac{1}{50}$				

of a dollar.   of a cwt.

m.	cts.
5	= $\frac{1}{2}$
2	$\frac{1}{5}$
1	$\frac{1}{10}$

of a ct.

CASE I.

When the price is $\frac{1}{4}$, $\frac{1}{2}$, $\frac{1}{3}$, $\frac{2}{3}$, or $\frac{3}{4}$ of a cent per article,
pound, yard, acre, bushel, &c.

RULE.

Divide the given sum or quantity by the aliquot parts of
a cent for the answer in cents.

EXAMPLES

1. What is the value of 124 apples at $\frac{1}{4}$ of a cent each?
2. What is the value of 1260 peaches at $\frac{1}{2}$ cent each?

$\frac{1}{4}$ | $\frac{1}{4}$ | 124 $\frac{1}{2}$ | $\frac{1}{2}$ | 1260

Ans.   31 cents. —   Ans. $6 30 cents.

3. What is the value of 192 plums, at $\frac{3}{4}$ of a cent each?
Ans. $1 44 cts.

4. What is the value of 24 quills, at $\frac{1}{3}$ of a cent each?
Ans. 8 cents.

5. What is the value of 12 cherries, at $\frac{2}{3}$ of a cent?
Ans. 8 cents.

6. How much will 29 come to, at $\frac{1}{4}$ of a cent each?
Ans. $7\frac{1}{4}$ cents.

7 How much will 11 come to, at $\frac{3}{4}$ of a cent each?
Ans. $8\frac{1}{4}$ cents.

8. What is the value of 19, at $\frac{1}{2}$ cent each?
Ans. $9\frac{1}{2}$ cents.

9. What is the value of 20, at 2 mills each?
Ans. 4 cents.

10. What is the value of 40, at 5 mills each?
Ans. 20 cents.

11. What is the value of 30, at 1 mill each?   Ans. 3 cts.

CASE 2.

When the given price is cents:

RULE.

Divide the given sum by the aliquot parts of a dollar for the answer in dollars.

EXAMPLES.

1. What is the value of 3216, at $6\frac{1}{4}$ cents?
2. What is the value of 8620, at 10 cents?

$6\frac{1}{4}$ | $\frac{1}{16}$ | 3216 (Ans. $201.
 32
 ───
  16
  16

10 | $\frac{1}{10}$ | 8620
Ans. $862

			$	cts.	m.
3. What is the value of 4260, at 20 cts.? Ans.			852	00	0
4.	8264,	20	1652	80	0
5.	4264,	$12\frac{1}{4}$	533	00	0
6.	5876,	50	2938	00	0
7	386,	25	96	50	0
8.	18626,	55	10244	30	0

6*

		$	cts.m.
9 What is the value of 3542, at 45 cts. ? Ans.		1593	90 0
10.	1724, 37½	646	50 0
11.	31925, 80	25540	00 0
12.	3654, 18¾	685	12 5
13.	13854, 56¼	7792	87·5

CASE 3.

When the given price is dollars and cents:

RULE.

Multiply the given sum by the dollars, and take parts for the cents, and add the products together for the answer in dollars.

EXAMPLES.

1. What is the value of 420 bushels of wheat, at 1 dollar 20 cents per bushel?

$$20 \mid \tfrac{1}{5} \mid \begin{array}{r} 420 \\ 1 \\ \hline 420 \\ 84 \\ \hline 504 \ \text{dollars.} \end{array}$$

		$ cts.		$	cts.m.
2. What is the value of 2412, at 2 06¼cts. ? Ans.				4974	75 0
3.	1224,	3 12½		3825	00 0
4.	870,	1 18¾		1033	12 5
5.	197,	4 20		827	40 0
6.	162,	2 25		364	50 0
7	217,	5 37½		1166	37 5
8.	1228,	7 62½		9363	50 0

CASE 4.

When the given sum consists of several denominations, such as yd., qr., na., &c. :

RULE.

Set down the given price of one of the highest denomination, and multiply it by the whole of the highest denomina-

tion given; then take aliquot parts of the next lowest de
nomination, continually, and add the products together for
the answer.

EXAMPLES.

1. What is the value of 10cwt. 2qr. 7lb. at $10 25 cents
per cwt.?

qr.		$ cts.
2	½	10 25
lb.		10 cwt.
7	1/16	
		102 50
		5 12½
		64

Ans. $108 26½ cts. +

2. What is the value of 5cwt. 1qr. 14lb., at 2 dollars 50
cents per cwt.? ▸ Ans. $13 43¾ cents.

3. What is the value of 7cwt. 3qr. 19lb., at 4 dollars 15
cents per cwt.? Ans. $32 86¼ cents.

4. What is the value of 780bu. 3pe. 2qt., at 1 dollar 17
cts. per bushel? Ans. $913 55 cents +

5. What is the value of 129cwt. 1qr. 10lb., at 1 dollar
5 cents per cwt.? Ans. $135 80 6m. +

6. What is the value of 25cwt. 1qr. 9lb., at 1 dollar 75
cents per cwt.? Ans. $44 32 cents. +

7. What is the value of 2qr. 14lb., at $27 10 cents per
cwt.? Ans. $16 93¾ cents.

8. What is the value of 12cwt. 3qr., at $40 20 cents per
cwt.? Ans. $512 55 cents.

9. What is the value of 19bu. 1pe. of corn, at 35 cts. per
bushel? Ans. 6 dollars 73¾ cents.

10. What is the value of 816 ounces 13dwt. 12gr., at
12½ cents per ounce? Ans. 102 dollars 8¼ cents

11. What is the value of 27yds. 3qr., at $9 65 cents per
yard? Ans. 267 dollars 78cts. 7m.

12. What is the value of 860yds. 1q., at 84 cents per
yard? Ans. 722 dollars 61 cents.

13. What is the value of 126yds. 2qr. 2na., at 4 dollars
75 cents per yard? Ans. 601 dollars 46cts. 8m. +

14. What is the value of 17hhd. 15gal. 3qt., at 64 dollars 75 cents per hhd.? Ans. 1116 dollars 93cts. 7m.

INTEREST

Interest is a consideration allowed for the use of money, relative to which are 4 particulars, viz: Principal, Time, Rate per Cent. and Amount. The principal is the money for which interest is to be received; the rate per cent. per annum is the interest of 100 dollars for one year; the time is the number of years or months, &c., for which interest is to be calculated; the amount is the principal and interest added together.

CASE 1.

To find the interest for any number of years, or years and months.

RULE.

Multiply the principal, consisting of dollars, by the rate per cent., and that product by the number of years; or if there be months, take aliquot parts of a year, cut off two figures on the right of the product for cents; or if there be cents in the principal, cut off one figure on the right as a remainder; one more for mills; two more for cents; those on the left will be dollars.

CASE 2.

To find the interest for any number of months.

RULE.

Find the interest at 6 per cent., by multiplying the principal by half the number of months; or at any other per cent., find the interest at 6; then state, if 6 give that interest, what will the per cent. you wish to calculate give, and cut off figures in the product for cents, as in Case 1st.

CASE 3.

To find the interest for any number of days.

RULE.

Multiply the principal by the number of days; divide the product by 6, the quotient will be the interest in mills at 6 per cent. If the principal consist of dollars and cents, destroy 2 figures on the right of the product; the balance will be the interest as before. If any other per cent. is required, take aliquot parts and add or subtract, according as the per cent. is more or less than 6.

Note. Case 3d is estimating 360 days in a year, which will make the interest rather large; it may be more accurately found by multiplying the principal by the number of days, and dividing the product by a proper divisor in the following table, which divisors are found by the following stating:

per cent. $ da.   per cent. $ da.
Thus: 4 : 100 : : 365.   Again, thus : 5 : 100 : : 365

Rate per cent.	Divisors.	Rate per cent.	Divisors.
4	9125	7.	5214
4½	8111	7½	4866
5	7300	8	4562
5½	6636	8½	4294
6	6083	9	4055
6½	5615	9½	3842
0	0000	10	3650

A divisor may also be found for weeks or months, by using 52 weeks or 12 months in room of 365 days.

CASE 1.

EXAMPLES.

1. What is the interest of $500 for 1 year, at 6 per cent. per annum?
2. What is the interest of 40 dollars 50 cents for one year and six months, at six per cent. per annum?

```
        $                              $    cts.
       500                            40    50
         6                                    6
     _____      months.|  |    _____
 Ans. $30|00cts.        6    |½ | 243    00
                             |  |          1
                                    _____
                                    243    00
                                    121    50
                                    _____
                             Ans. $3 64 cts. 5m.
```

3. What is the interest of 400 dollars for one year, at six per cent.? Ans. 24 dollars.

4. What is the interest of 600 dollars for one year, at six per cent. per annum? Ans. 36 dollars.

5. What is the interest of 250 dollars for one year, at five per cent.? Ans. 12 dollars 50 cents.

6. What is the interest of 51 dollars for one year, at six per cent.? Ans. 3 dollars 6 cents.

7. What is the interest of 44 dollars for two years, at seven per cent. per annum? Ans. 6 dollars 16 cts.

8. What is the interest of 90 dollars for three years, at five per cent.? Ans. 13 dollars 50 cents.

9. What is the interest of 68 dollars for four years, at four per cent.? Ans. 10 dollars 88 cents.

10. What is the interest of 1000 dollars for four years, at eight per cent.? Ans. 320 dollars.

11. What is the interest of 50 dollars for five years, at five per cent.? Ans. 12 dollars 50 cents.

12. What is the interest of 10 dollars for two years, at four per cent.? Ans. 1 dollar 52 cents.

13. What will be the interest of 1772 dollars for two years, at six per cent.? Ans. 212 dollars 64 cents.

14. How much interest will 75 dollars draw in five years, at 4½ per cent.? Ans. 16 dollars 87½ cts.

15. What is the interest of 100 dollars for two years and six months, at 6 per cent. per annum? Ans. 15 dollars.

16. What will be the interest of 350 dollars for three years and four months, at 6 per cent. per annum?
Ans. 70 dollars.

17 What will be the interest of 48 dollars for four years and one month, at 5 per cent. per annum?
Ans. 9 dollars 80 cents.

18. What is the interest of 64 dollars for one year and seven months, at 7 per cent. per annum?
Ans. 7 dollars 9⅓ cents.

19. What is the interest of 14 dollars for four years and 11 months, at 7 per cent.? Ans. 4 dollars 81¼ cts.

CASE 2.

EXAMPLES.

1. What is the interest of 40 dollars for four months, at 6 per cent. per annum? Ans. 80 cents.

2. What is the interest of 60 dollars for 6 months, at 8 per cent. per annum?   Ans. 2 dollars 40 cts.

$$
\begin{array}{c}
\$ \\
40 \\
2 \\
\hline
80 \text{ cents}
\end{array}
\qquad\qquad
\begin{array}{c}
\$ \\
60 \\
3 \\
\hline
6 : 8 : : 180 \\
8 \\
\hline
6)1440 \\
\hline
\$2\ 40
\end{array}
$$

3. What is the interest of 18 dollars for six months, at six per cent. per annum?   Ans. $0 54 cents.

4. What is the interest of 50 dollars for eight months, at seven per cent. per annum?   Ans. $2 33⅓ cts.

5. What is the interest of $900 for five months, at five per cent. per annum?   Ans. 18 dollars 75 cts.

6. What is the interest of 91 dollars 50 cents for four months, at 4 per cent.?   Ans. 1 dollar 22 cents.

7. What is the interest of 80 dollars for five months, at seven per cent.?   Ans. 2 dollars 33⅓ cents.

Note. When the amount is required, add the interest to the principal.

8. What is the amount of $62 50 cents for thirteen months, at 6 per cent. per annum?   Ans. $66 56cts. 5m.

9. What is the interest of $75 for fourteen months, at six per cent.?   Ans. 5 dollars 25 cents.

10. What is the interest of $5 50 cents for 5¼ months, at six per cent.?   Ans. 15 cents. +

Note. In this case, after finding the interest at six per cent., if any other rate per cent. be required, take aliquot parts and add or subtract, according as the rate per cent. is more or less than six.

11. What is the interest of 80 dollars for eight months, at five per cent.?

12. What is the interest of 60 dollars for four months, at eight per cent. ?

```
6 per.                    8
5 per.          $         6              $
 —                        —             60
1              80         2              2
               4                    2 | ½ | 1 20 int. at 6 per ct.
        1 | ½ | 320 int. at 6 per ct.      40
               53¼                      ————————
       ———————                          $1·60 cents.
```

Ans. $2 66⅔

13. What is the interest of 120 dollars 60 cents for fifteen months, at 6 per cent. ?   Ans. 9 dollars 4cts. 5m.

14. What is the interest of 5420 dollars for 17 months, at 4 per cent. per annum ?   Ans. 307 dollars 13⅓ cts.

15. What is the interest of 7200 dollars for 14 months, at 6 per cent. per annum ?   Ans. 504 dollars.

16. What is the interest of 8050 dollars 87½ cents for 47 months, at 6 per cent. per annum ?
       • Ans. 1891 dollars 95cts. 5m.

17. What is the interest of 948 dollars 62½ cents for eight months, at 8 per cent. per annum ?
       Ans. 50 dollars 59 cents. +

18. What is the interest of 36 dollars for one month, at 8 per cent. per annum ?   Ans. 24 cents.

19. What is the interest of ·1000 dollars for 40 months, at 6 per cent. per annum ?   Ans. 200 dollars.⸱

20. What is the interest of 328 dollars for 12 months, at 6 per cent. ?   Ans. 19 dollars 68 cents.

When there is a fraction in the rate per cent., as 5½, 6½, or 6¾, multiply and add ¼ or ½, (as the case may be,) of the principal to the product, and proceed as before.

21. What will be the interest of 540 dollars for 24 months, at 5 per cent. per annum ?   Aus. 54 dollars.

22. What would be the interest of 482 dollars for 84 months, at 6 dollars per cent. per annum ?
       Ans. 202 dollars 44 cts.

23. What is the interest of 325 dollars for 50 months, at 4 per cent. per annum?   Ans. $54 16 cents 6m.

24. What is the interest of 840 dollars for 63 months, at 4 per cent. per annum?   Ans. $176 40 cents.

25. What is the interest of 840 dollars for 64 months, at 7 per cent. per annum?   Ans. $313 60 cents.

26. What is the interest of 560 dollars for 4 months, at six per cent. per annum?   Ans. $11 20 cents.

27. What is the interest and amount of 100 dollars for ten months, at 10 per cent. per annum?

Answer. $\left\{ \begin{array}{l} \$8\ 33\frac{1}{3}\ \text{interest.} \\ \$108\ 33\frac{1}{3}\ \text{amount.} \end{array} \right.$

28. What is the amount of 76 dollars 25 cents for 25 months, at 6 per cent. per annum?   Ans. $85 78cts. 1m. +

CASE 3.

Note. Multiply any principal by the rate per cent., and that product by the number of days it has been on interest, and divide the last product by 365. The quotient will be the interest.

EXAMPLES.

1. What is the interest of 1000 dollars for five days, at 6 per cent. per annum?   Ans. 83 cents 3m. +

2. What is the interest of 500 dollars for 60 days, at 8 per cent. per annum?   Ans. $6 66cts. 6m. +

$$\begin{array}{r} \$ \\ 1000 \\ 5 \\ \hline 6)5000 \\ \hline 83|3\frac{1}{3} \end{array}$$

$$\begin{array}{r} \$ \\ 500 \\ 60 \\ \hline 6)30000 \\ \hline 2\ |\ \frac{1}{3}\ |\ 5000 \\ 1666\frac{2}{3} \\ \hline 6|66|6\frac{2}{3} \end{array}$$

3. What is the interest of 400 dollars for 40 days, at 6 per cent. per annum?   Ans. $2 66cts. 6m. +

4. What is the interest of 900 dollars for fourteen days, at 6 per cent.?   Ans. $2 10 cents.

5. What is the interest of 1000 dollars for 4 days, at 6 per cent.?   Ans. 66⅔ cents.

6. What is the interest of 500 dollars for one day, at 6 per cent.?   Ans. 8 cents 3m. +

7. What is the interest of 16 dollars 33⅓ cents for 24 days, at 6 per cent.?   Ans. 6 cents 5m. +

8. What is the interest of 64 dollars 64 cents for 18 days at 6 per cent. per annum?   Ans. 19 cents 3m.

9. What is the interest of 45 dollars for 22 days, at 5½ per cent. per annum?   Ans. 15 cents. +

10. What is the interest of 90 dollars for 51 days, at 8 per cent. per annum?   Ans. 1 dollar 2 cents.

Note. When the time is years, months, and days, proceed with the years and months as in Case 1st, and for the days take aliquot parts of 30.

11. What is the interest of 50 dollars for 1 year, 2 months, and 5 days, at 6 per cent. per annum?   Ans. $3 54 cents.

12. What is the interest of 100 dollars for one year, 7 months, and 11 days, at 6 per cent.?   Ans. $9 68 cents. +

13. What is the interest of 21 dollars for 4 years, 4 months, and 4 days, at 5 per cent.?   Ans. $4 56 cents. +

14. What is the interest of 5 dollars for 10 years, 3 months, and 19 days, at 6 per cent.?   Ans. $3 09 cents. +

15. What is the interest of 5 dollars 87½ cents for 9 months, and 24 days, at 6 per cent. per annum?
                                        Ans. 28 cents 7m. +

CASE 4.

The **amount, time and rate per cent.** given to find the principal.

RULE.

Find the amount of 100 dollars at the rate per cent. and time given, which amount is the first term; the given sum the 2d; 100 dollars the 3d; proceed by the Rule of Three; the quotient will be the principal required.

EXAMPLES.

1. What principal at interest for 8 years, at 5 per cent., will amount to 840 dollars?

$$140 : 840 : : 100$$
$$100$$

$$\begin{array}{r} \$ \\ 100 \\ 5 \\ \hline 500 \\ 8 \\ \hline \end{array}$$

14|0)8400|0(Ans. $600.
84

Interest. 40|00
100

00

Amount. 140

2. What principal at interest for 5 years, at 6 per cent. per annum, will amount to 650 dollars?   Ans. $500.
3. What principal at interest for 5 years, at 6 per cent. per annum, will amount to 2470 dollars?   Ans. $1900.

CASE 5.

To find the rate per cent. when the amount, time and principal are given.

RULE.

Subtract the principal from the amount; then state if the principal give the interest or remainder, what will 100 dollars give. Divide the answer by the number of years; the quotient will be the rate per cent.

1. At what rate per cent. per annum will $500 amount to $650 in five years?

	$		$	$	$
Amount.	650	500	:	100	150
Principal.	500			150	
	150 interest.			5000	
				100	

50|0)150|00
Years. 5)30

Ans. 6 per cent.

2. At what rate per cent. will 600 dollars amount to $744 in four years?   Ans. 6 per cent.

4. If 834 dollars, at interest 2 years and 6 months, amount to $927 82½ cts., what was the rate per cent. per annum?   Ans. 4½ per cent.

CASE 6.

To find the time when the principal, amount, and rate per cent. are given.

RULE.

Divide the whole interest by the interest of the principal for one year.   The quotient will be the time required.

1. In what time will 400 dollars amount to 520 dollars, at 5 per cent. per annum?

$	$
400	520
5	400
20|00	2|0)12|0

Ans. 6 years.

2. In what time will 600 dollars amount to 798, at 6 per cent. per annum?   Ans. 5½ years.

3. Suppose 1000 dollars, at 4½ per cent. per annum, amount to 1281 dollars 25 cts., how long was it at interest?   Ans. 6 years 3 months.

PROMISCUOUS EXAMPLES,

1. What is the interest of 500 dollars for one year and 2 months, at 6 per cent. ?   Ans. 35 dollars.

2. What is the interest of 450 dollars for 2 years and 6 months, at 5 per cent. per annum?   Ans. 56 dollars 25 cts.

3. What is the interest of 65 dollars 87½ cents for 9 months, at 6 per cent. ?   Ans. 2 dollars 96¼ cts.

4. What is the interest of 800 dollars for four years, 5 months and 19 days, at 6 per cent. per annum?
                    Ans. 214 dollars 58cts. 3m. +

5. What is the interest of 18 dollars 75 cts. for 1 year, 2 months and 7 days, at 6 per cent. per annum?
                    Ans. 1 dollar 33⅓ cents.

6. What is the interest of 90 dollars for 8 months, at 9 per cent.?   Ans. 5 dollars 40 cts.

7 What is the interest of 6 dollars for 6 days, at 6 per cent.?   Ans. 6 mills.

8. What is the amount of 1000 dollars 25 cts. for 4 years, 4 months, and 5 days, at 7½ per cent. per annum?
                    Ans. 1326 dollars 37 cts. 3m.+

9. In what time will 1000 dollars amount to 1500 dollars, at 8 per cent. per annum?   Ans. 6 years 3 months.

10. What is the interest of 25 cts. for 25 years, at 6 per cent. per annum?   Ans. 37½ cts.

11. What is the interest of 87½ cents for 1 year and 6 months, at 6 per cent. per annum?   Ans. 7 cts. 8m.+

12. At what rate per cent. per annum will 1200 dollars amount to 1800 dollars in 5 years?   Ans. 10 per ct.

INSURANCE, COMMISSION, AND BROKERAGE.

Brokerage is an allowance to insure factors and brokers at a stipulated rate per cent., agreed on by the parties concerned.

RULE.

Multiply the sum by the rate per cent. If the rate be less than one per cent., take aliquot parts.

EXAMPLES.

1. What is the commission on 500 dollars, at 5 per cent.?

2. What is the commission on 400 dollars, at ¾ dollars per cent.?

$
\begin{array}{r}
\$ \\
500 \\
5 \\
\hline
\text{Ans. } \$25\ 00
\end{array}
\qquad
\begin{array}{cc|r}
\frac{1}{2} & \frac{1}{2} & \$\ 400 \\
 & & \hline \\
\frac{1}{4} & \frac{1}{4} & 200 \\
 & & 100 \\
\hline
& & \text{Ans. } \$3\ 00
\end{array}
$

3. What is the insurance of 60 dollars, at 3 per cent.?
Ans. 1 dollar 80 cents.

4. What is the commission on 1351 dollars 50 cents, at 5½ per cent.? Ans. 74 dollars 33 cents. +

5. The sales of certain goods amount to 1680 dollars, what sum is to be received for them, allowing 2¼ per cent. for commission? Ans. 1638 dollars 80 cents.

6. What is the commission on 3450 dollars, at 4½ per cent.? Ans. 155 dollars 25 cents.

7 When a broker sells goods to the amount of 984 dollars 50 cents, what is his commission, at 1¼ per cent.?
Ans. 12 dollars 30 cents 6m. +

8. What is the insurance of 1250 dollars, at 7½ per cent.?
Ans. 93 dollars 75 cents.

9. If a broker buys goods for me, amounting to 1650 dollars 75 cents, what sum must I pay him, allowing 1½ per cent.? Ans. 24 dollars 76 cents 1m. +

10. What is the commission on a sale of goods, amounting to 1184 dollars, at 5 per cent.? Ans. 59 dollars 20 cts.

11. What is the commission on a sale of goods, amounting to 4820 dollars, at 4½ per cent.?
Ans. 216 dollars 90 cents.

DISCOUNT

Discount is an allowance made for the payment of a sum of money before it becomes due, and is the difference between that sum due sometime hence and its present worth.

RULE.

Find the interest of 100 dollars at the per cent. and time given; to this interest add 100 dollars, which amount is the first term; the given sum the second; 100 dollars the third. Proceed by the Rule of Three. The answer will be the present worth. Subtract the answer from the given sum, and the remainder will be the discount.

EXAMPLES.

1. What is the discount of 500 dollars for 4 years, discount at 5 per cent. per annum?

$$\$$$
$$100$$
$$5$$
———
$$500$$
$$4$$
———
$$20|00$$
$$100$$
———
$$120 : 500 : : 100$$
$$100$$
———
$$12|0)500 0|0$$
———

present worth.   416 66¾

      $ cts.

      500   00

      416   66¾
———

Discount. $83 33⅓

2. What is the present worth of 600 dollars, due in 2 years, discount at 6 per cent. per annum?

                   Ans. $535 71cts. 4m. +

3. What is the discount of 590 dollars for 2 years, discount at 6 per cent. per annum?   Ans. $63 21½ cts.

4. What is the present worth of 480 dollars, due in 4 years, at 4 per cent. discount?   Ans. 413 dollars 79½cts. +

5. What is the discount of 645 dollars for 9 months, at 6 per cent. per annum?   Ans. $27 77cts. 6m.

6. What is the present worth of 580 dollars, due in 8 months, discount at 6 per cent. per annum?

                   Ans. 557 69 cents. +

7. What is the present worth of 775 dollars 50 cents, due in 4 years, at 5 per cent. per annum?

                   Ans. $646 25 cents.

8. Bought goods amounting to 615 dollars 75 cents, at 6 months' credit, how much ready money must be paid if a discount of 4½ per cent. be allowed?   Ans. $602 20 cts.

9. Bought goods amounting to 900 dollars, at 4 years' credit, how much ready money must be paid if a discount of 6 per cent. be allowed?   Ans. $725 80½ cents.

10. What is the discount of 90 dollars for 1 year and 6 months, at 6 per cent. per annum?　　　Ans. $7 43¼ cents.

11. What is the discount of 205 dollars, due in 15 months, at 7 per cent. per annum?　　Ans. $16 49½ cts. +

12. A. owes B. 100 dollars, due in one year, but B. agrees to allow A. a discount of 25 per cent. per annum for present payment. What sum will discharge the debt?
　　　　　　　　　　　　　　　　　Ans. 80 dollars.

13. What is the discount of 100 dollars, due in 12 months, at 25 per cent. per annum?　　Ans. 20 dollars.

Note. When discount is made without regard to time, it is found precisely like the interest for one year.

14. What is the discount of 800 dollars, at 6 per cent.?
15. What is the discount of 99 dollars, at 5 per cent.?

$$
\begin{array}{cc}
\$ & \$ \\
800 & 99 \\
6 & 5 \\
\hline
\end{array}
$$

Ans. $48 00 discount.　　　　　Ans. $4 95

16. What is the discount of 476 dollars, at 3 per cent.?
　　　　　　　　　　Ans. 14 dollars 28 cents.

TARE AND TRET

Tare and Tret are certain allowances made by merchants in selling their goods by weight. Tare is an allowance made for the weight of the barrel, box, &c., that contains the commodity bought. Tret is an allowance of 4 lb. in every 104 lb. for waste, dust, &c. Gross weight is the goods, together with the barrel, box, or whatever contains them. When the tare is deducted from the gross, what remains is called suttle. Neat weight is the weight of articles after all allowances are deducted.

RULE.

1st. Subtract the whole tare from the whole gross; the remainder will be neat. 2nd. When the tare is so much per barrel, box, &c., multiply the tare per barrel, box, &c.,

by the number of barrels, boxes, &c. The product will be the whole tare. Subtract the whole tare from the whole gross, and the remainder will be neat. 3d. When the tare is so much per cwt., run aliquot part, or parts of a cwt., through the whole gross. Subtract the quotient therefrom, and the remainder will be neat. 4th. When tret is allowed with tare, subtract the tare from the gross, as before. The remainder will be suttle. Divide the suttle by 26. The quotient will be tret. Subtract the tret from the suttle, and the remainder will be neat.

EXAMPLES.

1. What is the neat weight of a hogshead of tobacco, weighing 2cwt. 3qr. 25lb. gross, tare in all 1cwt. 2qr. 12lb.?

$$
\begin{array}{ccc}
cwt. & qr. & lb. \\
2 & 3 & 25 \text{ gross.} \\
1 & 2 & 12 \text{ tare.} \\
\hline
\text{Ans. } 1 & 1 & 13 \text{ neat.}
\end{array}
$$

2. What is the neat weight of a hogshead of tobacco, weighing 5cwt. 2qr. 15lb. gross, when the tare is 3qr. 7lb.?
Ans. 4cwt. 3qr. 8lb.

3. What is the neat weight of 369cwt. 2qrs. 21lb. gross, tare in the whole 10cwt. 1qr. 12lb.?
Ans. 359cwt. 1qr. 9lb.

4. What is the neat weight of 6 hogsheads of sugar, each weighing 4cwt. 1qr. 4lb. gross, tare in the whole 13cwt. 3qr. 19lb.?

$$
\begin{array}{ccc}
cwt. & qr. & lb. \\
4 & 1 & 4 \\
 & & 6 \\
\hline
25 & 2 & 24 \text{ whole gross weight.} \\
13 & 3 & 19 \text{ whole tare} \\
\hline
11 & 3 & 5 \text{ neat.}
\end{array}
$$

5. How much is the neat weight of 7 casks of indigo, each weighing 3cwt. 2qr. 12lb. gross, tare 25lb. per cask?

<table>
<tr><td colspan="3">cwt. qr. lb.</td><td></td><td colspan="3">cwt. qr. lb.</td></tr>
<tr><td>3</td><td>2</td><td>12</td><td></td><td>0</td><td>0</td><td>25</td></tr>
<tr><td></td><td></td><td>7</td><td></td><td></td><td></td><td>7</td></tr>
</table>

25	1	0	gross.	1	2	7	tare in all.
1	2	7					

Ans. 23 2 21 neat.

6. What is the neat weight of 6 casks of raisins, each weighing 3cwt. 2qr. 10lb. gross, tare 20lb. per cask?

Ans. 20cwt. 1qr. 24lb.

7. What is the neat weight of 35 kegs of figs, gross weight 37cwt. 1qr. 20lb., tare per cwt. 14lb.?

<table>
<tr><td></td><td></td><td>cwt.</td><td>qr.</td><td>lb.</td></tr>
<tr><td>lb.</td><td>⅛</td><td>37</td><td>1</td><td>20</td></tr>
<tr><td>14</td><td></td><td>4</td><td>2</td><td>20 quotient.</td></tr>
</table>

Ans. 32 3 00 neat.

8. What is the neat weight of 6 hogsheads of sugar, each weighing 7cwt. 3qr. 14lb. gross, tare 20lb. per cwt.?

Ans. 38cwt. 3qr. 7lb.

9. What is the neat weight and value of 12 bags of coffee, each 2cwt. 1qr. 10lbs. gross, tare 18lb. per cwt., tret 4lb. per 104lb., at 19 dollars 60 cents per cwt.?

Answer. { 22cwt. 2qr. 18lb. neat.
{ 444 dollars 15 cts. value.

10. What is the cost of 24 casks of prunes, each cask weighing 1cwt. 1qr. 23lb. gross, tare 18lb. per cask, at 5 dollars 17¾ cents per cwt.?   Ans. $160 79cts. 4m.

11. What is the neat weight of 5 hogsheads of sugar, each 10cwt. 1qr. 20lb. gross, tare 3qr. 25lb. per hogshead, tret 4lb. per 104lb.?

<table>
<tr><td colspan="3">cwt. qr. lb.</td><td></td><td colspan="3">cwt. qr. lb.</td></tr>
<tr><td>10</td><td>1</td><td>20</td><td></td><td>0</td><td>3</td><td>25</td></tr>
<tr><td></td><td></td><td>5</td><td></td><td></td><td></td><td>5</td></tr>
</table>

52	0	16	gross.	4	3	13	tare.
4	3	13	tare.				

Divide by 26)47 1 3 suttle.
            1 3 7 tret quotient.

Ans. 45 1 24 neat.

To find the neat weight of Pork, established by custom, when the gross is given.

RULE.

Place each hundred separately. Then subtract $\frac{1}{4}$ or 25 from the first hundred : $\frac{1}{8}$ or $12\frac{1}{2}$ from the second hundred. The remainders will be neat. All over the second hundred is neat. Add the remainders and all over the second hundred together for the neat.

Note. $\frac{1}{4}$ must be taken from any number of pounds gross, under 100 including : — $\frac{1}{8}$ from all over 100 pounds, and under 200 including.

EXAMPLES.

1. What is the neat of a hog weighing 184 pounds gross?
2. What is the neat of a hog weighing 212 pounds gross?

25	$\frac{1}{4}$	100 $12\frac{1}{2}$	$\frac{1}{8}$	84 25	$\frac{1}{4}$	100 $12\frac{1}{2}$	$\frac{1}{8}$	100 12
		25		$10\frac{1}{2}$		25		$12\frac{1}{2}$
		75		$73\frac{1}{2}$		75		$87\frac{1}{2}$
		$73\frac{1}{2}$				$87\frac{1}{2}$		
						12		

Ans. $148\frac{1}{2}$ Neat.

Ans. $174\frac{1}{2}$ Neat.

3. What is the neat of a hog weighing 305 pounds gross?
                  Ans. $267\frac{1}{2}$lb. neat.

4. What is the neat of 3 hogs weighing gross as follows, viz.: no. 1, 191 lb.; no. 2, 76 lb.; no. 3, 201 lb.?
                  Ans. $375\frac{1}{4}$ lb. neat.

5. What is the neat of 2 hogs weighing gross as follows, viz.: no. 1, 219 lb.; no. 2, 113 lb.?   Ans. 268 lbs. neat.

EQUATION

Equation is used to find the mean time of several payments due at different times.

RULE.

Multiply each payment by its time. Add up the several products, and divide the sum by the whole debt.

EXAMPLES.

1. A. owes B. 60 dollars, of which 40 dollars is to be paid at 6 months, and 20 dollars at 3 months, but they agree that the whole shall be paid at one time. When must it be paid?

$$40 \times 6 = 240$$
$$20 \times 3 = \ \ 60$$

$$6|0)30|0$$

Ans. 5 months.

2. C. owes D. 380 dollars, of which 100 dollars is to be paid at 6 months, 120 dollars at 7 months, and 160 dollars at 10 months, but they agree that the whole shall be paid at one time. When must it be paid? Ans. 8 months.

3. A merchant has owing to him 300 dollars, to be paid as follows, viz.: 100 dollars at 2 months; 100 dollars at 4 months; 100 dollars at 6 months; but they agree that the whole shall be paid at one time. When must it be paid?

Ans. 4 months.

4. A merchant has purchased goods to the amount of 2000 dollars, of which sum 400 dollars are to be paid at present, 800 dollars at 6 months, and the rest at 9 months; but it is agreed to make one payment of the whole. When must it be paid? Ans. 6 months.

5. A. owes J. 500 dollars, which will be due four months hence. It is agreed that 100 dollars shall be paid now, and that the rest remain unpaid a longer time than four months. When must it be paid? Ans. 5 months.

6. A. owes B. 100 dollars, of which 75 dollars is to be paid at 4 months, and 25 dollars at 2 months; but they agree that the whole shall be paid at one time. When must it be paid? Ans. $3\frac{1}{2}$ months.

7 C. is indebted to a merchant to the amount of 2500 dollars, of which 1000 dollars is payable at the end of 4 months, 800 dollars in 8 months, and 700 dollars in 12 months; when ought payment to be made if all are paid together? Ans. $7\frac{1}{2}$ months. +

BARTER.

Barter is the exchanging of one commodity for another, according to a certain price or value agreed on by the parties concerned. Questions in Barter may be solved by the Rule of Three.

When any articles, at a given price per article, are to be bartered for any other articles, at a given price per article.

RULE.

Find the value of the articles whose quantity is given. Then find how many of the other articles may be bought with that money.

EXAMPLES.

1. A. has 400 yards of cloth, at 20 cents per yard, for which B. is to give him books, at 50 cents each. How many books must A. receive?

2. C. has 100 bushels of wheat, at 75 cents per bushel, for which D. is to give him rye, at $37\frac{1}{2}$ cents per bushel. How many bushels of rye ought C. to receive?

cts.	cts.	yd.		cts.	cts.	bu.	

$$50 : 20 : : 400$$
$$400$$
$$5|0)800|0$$
Ans. 160 books.

$$37\frac{1}{2} : 75 : : 100$$
$$2 \qquad 2$$
$$75 \qquad 150$$
$$100$$
$$75)15000(\text{Ans. } 200 \text{ bu.}$$
$$150$$
$$00$$

3. M. has 500 barrels of flour, at 6 dollars per barrel, for which R. is to give him salt, at 1 dollar 25 cents per bushel. How many bushels of salt ought M. to receive?
Ans. 2400 bu.

4. A. has 20 pounds of sugar, at $12\frac{1}{2}$ cents per pound, for which J. is to give him fowls, at 10 cents a piece. How many fowls ought A. to receive? Ans. 25 fowls.

5. How many bushels of rye, at 40 cents per bushel, are equal to 90 bushels of wheat, at 50 cents per bushel?
Ans. 112½bu.

6. G. has 160 yards of stuff, at 14 cents per yard, for which N. agrees to give him oats, at 20 cents per bushel. How many bushels of oats ought G. to receive?
Ans. 112bu.

7. P. sold 108 yards of calico, at 10 cents per yard, for which E. gave him 6 dollars in money, and the rest in flaxseed, at 8 cents per bushel. How many bushels of flaxseed did P. receive?   Ans. 60bu.

8. How many pounds of tea, at 30 cents per pound, must be given in barter for 25 pounds of coffee, at 22½ cents per pound?   Ans. 18¾ pounds.

9. A merchant has 1000 yards of canvass, at 20 cents per yard, which he is to barter for serge, at 22½ cents per yard. How many yards of serge should he receive?
Ans. 888 4/9 yards.

10. A. has sugar at 12½ cents per pound, for a quantity of which C. is to give him 450 pounds of tea, at 1 dollar per pound. How much sugar must C. receive?
Ans. 3600 pounds.

11. H. has 1000 bushels of salt, at 1 dollar 10 cents per bushel; for which W is to give him 80 gallons of brandy, at 87½ cents per gallon, and the rest in cotton, at 15 cents per pound. How many pounds of cotton must H. receive?
Ans. 6866⅔ pounds.

12. What quantity of candles, at $9 50 cents per cwt., must be given for 15cwt 0qr. 27lb, of tobacco, at 20 cents per pound?   Ans. 35cwt. 3qr. 20lb. +

13. Two persons barter — A. has 17cwt. of iron, at 13½ cents per lb. — B. has 1200lb. of cheese, at 14 dollars per cwt. — which of them must receive money, and how much?
Ans. A. 107 dollars 4 cents.

14. E. has 2108lb. of bacon, at 10 cents per pound, and 31 bushels of apples, at 11½ cents per bushel, which he barters with F. thus: E. to have 135 dollars 25 cents in money, and the rest in pork, at 1 dollar 58 cents per barrel. How many barrels is he to receive?   Ans. 50 barrels. +

15. K. bought of Y 102lb. of lard, at 8¼ cents per pound, and is to pay him as follows, viz: in cash 1 dollar 1 cent, 20 lb. of leather, at 20 cents per pound, and 40 pounds

of beef, at 2¼ cents per pound, and the rest in butter, at 6¼
cents per pound. How many pounds of butter must Y
receive?   Ans. 39$\frac{21}{25}$ pounds

LOSS AND GAIN.

Loss and gain is used to show how much is gained or lost
in dealing.

RULE.

1st. Subtract the cost from the sale; the remainder will
be the gain.   Or, if the cost be more than the sale, subtract
the sale from the cost, and the remainder will be the loss.
2d. When you wish to sell any commodity at a certain gain
per cent., and wish to know what sum it must be sold for,
say; if 100 give 100 with the per cent. added, what will the
first cost give? 3d. When the amount is given at a certain
rate gain per cent., to find the first cost, say; if 100, with
the rate per cent. added, give 100, what will the amount
give?   4th. When any commodity is sold at a certain rate
per cent. loss, to find the sum received, say; if 100 give 100
less the per cent. lost, what will the first cost give?

EXAMPLES.

1. What will a merchant gain by buying 95 bushels of
salt, at 1 dollar 20 cents per bushel, and selling it again, at
1 dollar 50 cents per bushel?

$ cts.
1 50   95 bushels
1 20   30

Gain on one bushel, 30·   Ans. $28 50 cents.

2. Bought 55 yards of cloth, at 13 cents per yard, and
sold the same again for 15 cents per yard.   How much was
gained by the transaction?   Ans. $1 10 cts.
3. If I buy 50 yards of cloth, at 25 cents per yard, and
sell the same again for 30 cents per yard, how much do I
gain?   Ans. 2 dollars 50 cents.
4. If I buy 100 yards of tape, at 20 cents per yard, and
sell it for 18 cents per yard, how much do I lose in the
transaction?   Ans. 2 dollars.

5. If I buy 40 saddles, at 11 dollars 50 cents each, and sell them again at 10 dollars 99 cents; how much do I lose by the sale? Ans. 20 dollars 40 cts.

6. Bought 12 bushels of corn, at 22¼ cents per bushel, and sold it again at 22 cents per bushel. How much did I lose by the transaction? Ans. 6 cents.

7. A man bought flour, at $5 per barrel, and sold it at $5 25 cents per barrel. How much did he gain on 363 barrels? ● Ans. 90 dollars 75 cts.

8. If I lay out 500 dollars in cloth, at 5 cents per yard, and sell the same again at 12¼ cents per yard, how much do I gain? Ans. 750 dollars.

9. If I buy a horse for 60 dollars, at how much must I sell him to gain 20 per cent.?

If 100 : 60 : : 120. Ans $72.

10. If I buy 100 yards of cloth for $50, at how much must I sell it per yard to gain 20 per cent. by the whole? Ans. 60 cents.

11. If I buy 54 yards of muslin for 29 dollars 84 cents, and sell the same again at 60 cents per yard, how much do I gain? Ans. 2 dollars 56 cents.

12. If I buy 90 horses for 1800 dollars, at how much must I sell each horse to gain 180 dollars in the whole? Ans. 22 dollars.

13. A merchant sold 40 yards of cloth, at 20 cents per yard, and by so doing gained 10 per cent. What was the first cost of each yard? Ans. 18 cents.+

$$40$$
$$20$$
$$\overline{}$$
$$110 : 800 : : 100$$
$$100$$

$$11|0)8000|0$$

Yards $4|0)72|7\frac{1}{2}$

$$18+$$

14. Bought a quantity of tea for $250, and sold it for 275 dollars. What is the gain, and gain per cent.? Ans. 25 dollars gained, 10 per cent.

15. Bought 490 bushels of corn for 326 dollars, and sold the same for 370 dollars 10 cents. What was the profit on each bushel? Ans. 9 cents.

16. Bought a parcel of goods for 60 dollars, and sold the same immediately for 90 dollars, with 6 months' credit How much per cent. per annum was gained?
Ans. 100 per cent

17. When a broker receives in exchange 5 cents per dollar profit, how much is the gain per cent.? Ans. $5.

18. A man purchased 7 pieces of cloth, at $13 75 cents per piece; but finding it somewhat damaged, he paid $3 12¼ cents per piece for dyeing it. At how much must each piece be sold to gain 12 per cent. on the whole?
Ans. $18 90 cents.

19. A trader bought 250 barrels of flour, at $4 50 cents a barrel. How must he sell each barrel to gain 100 dollars by the bargain? Ans. $4 90 cents.

20. If I purchase 16 pieces of cloth at 14 dollars per piece, and sell 5 pieces at 17 dollars per piece, and 6 at 15 dollars per piece, what must I sell the rest at per piece to gain 12 per cent. on the whole? Ans. $15 17cts. 6m.

PARTNERSHIP

Partnership is a joint interest or property, the union of two or more persons in the same trade, by which rule, persons in company trading together, are enabled to make a just division of the gain or loss, in proportion to each man's stock.

When the respective stocks have no time—

RULE.

Add the several shares together, which amount is the first term: either person's share, the 2nd.; the whole gain or loss, the 3rd. Proceed by the Rule of Three. 2nd. When the respective stocks have time, multiply each man's stock by its time. Add the several products together, which amount is the first term; either particular product, the 2nd.; the whole gain or loss, the 3rd. Proceed as before.

PROOF. Add together all the shares of gain or loss.

EXAMPLES.

1. A. B. and C. made a stock. A. put in $20, B $30, C. $40, and by trading, they gained 36 dollars. What was each man's share of the gain?

$$A. \ 20$$
$$B. \ 30$$
$$C. \ 40$$
$$\overline{}$$

Amount. 90 : 20 : : 36.   Ans. A.'s share $8.
90 : 30 : : 36.   Ans. B.'s share $12.
90 : 40 : : 36.   Ans. C.'s share $16.

Proof. $36.

2. A. and B. purchased goods worth 80 dollars; of which A. pays 30 dollars and B. 50 dollars. They gained 20 dollars; what is the gain of each?
Ans. A. $7 50 cts.   B. $12 50 cts.

3. Three merchants trading together gained $500. A.'s stock was $800; B.'s stock $700; C.'s stock $500. What was each man's share of the gain?
Ans. A.'s share $200; B.'s $175; C.'s $125.

4. A merchant being deceased, worth 1800 dollars, is found to owe the following sums : — To A. $1200; to B. $500; to C. $700. How much is each to have, in proportion to the debt? Ans. A. $900; B. $375; and C. $525.

5. B. C. and D. made a stock, by which they gained 800 dollars; whereof B.'s stock was 400 dollars; C.'s 500 dollars; and D.'s 600 dollars. I demand each man's share of the gain. Ans. B.'s $213⅓; C.'s $266⅔; D.'s $320.

6. Three drovers pay among them $60 for pasture, into which they put 200 cattle; of which A. had 50; B. 80; C. 70. I would know how much each had to pay?
Ans. A. $15; B. $24; C. $21.

7 Four men formed a capital of 3200 dollars. They gained in a certain time 6560 dollars. A.'s stock was 560 dollars; B.'s 1040 dollars; C.'s 1200 dollars; and D.'s 400 dollars. What did each gain?
Ans. A.'s $1143; B.'s 2132; C.'s 2460; and D.'s $820.

8. B. C. and D. traded together; B. put in 50 dollars for four months; C. 100 dollars for 6 months; and D. 150

dollars for 8 months. They gained 126 dollars 80 cts.; what is each man's share of the gain?

$ m.

B. 50 × 4 = 200
C. 100 × 6   600
D. 150 × 8   1200
———

		$ cts.			$ cts.
2000 :	200 ::	126 80	•	⎧	12 68 B.
2000 :	600 ::	126 80	Ans. ⎨		38 04 C.
2000 :	1200 ::	126 80	⎩		76 08 D.

9. O. P. and R. traded together; O. put in 100 dollars for 2 months, P. 200 dollars for four months, and R. 400 dollars for 5 months, and by trading together they gained 600 dollars 50 cents. How much is each man's gain in proportion to his stock?

Ans. ⎧ O. 40 dollars 3⅓ cents.
⎨ P. 160 dollars 13⅓ cents.
⎩ R. 400 dollars 33⅓ cents.

10. A. and W made a stock; A. put in 500 dollars for 6 months, and W 2000 dollars for 8 months, and by trading they gained 2600 dollars. I demand each man's share of the gain?

Ans. ⎧ A.   410 dollars 52 cents 5m. +
⎨ W. 2189 dollars 47 cents 3m. +

11. S. G. and W made a stock for 12 months; S. put in at first 500 dollars, and two months after he put in 40 dollars more; G. put in at first 805 dollars 50 cents, and at the end of ten months he took out 300 dollars; W put in at first 600 dollars 25 cents, and 4 months after he put in 100 dollars, and 6 months after that he put in 50 dollars 50 cents more. At the expiration of 12 months their gain is 1800 dollars 50 cents; what is each man's share of the gain?

Ans. ⎧ S. $488 89 cents 2m.
⎨ G. $692 54 cents 7m.
⎩ W $619 06 cents 0m.

———

EXCHANGE.

TABLES OF MONEY.

ENGLISH MONEY.

The denominations are,

4 farthings (marked qr.) make .	1 penny.	d.
12 pence.	1 shilling.	s.
20 shillings.	1 pound.	£.

TABLE,

Showing the value of English Money in Federal Money

New York and North Carolina.				South Carolina and Georgia.				New Jersey, Pennsylvania, Delaware, and Maryland.				N. Hampshire, Massachusetts, Rhode Island, Connecticut, Virginia, Kentucky, and Tennessee.			
s.	*d.*	$	*cts.*	*s.*	*d.*	$	*cts.*	*s.*	*d.*	$	*cts.*	*s.*	*d.*	$	*cts.*
	2		2		2		3½		2		2		2		2¾
	3		3		3		5⅓		3		3⅓		3		4
	4		4		4		7		4		4⅓		4		5½
	4½		4⅔		4½		8		4½		5		4½		6¼
	6		6¼		6		10⅔		6		6⅔		6		8⅓
	9		9⅓		9		16		9		10		9		12½
1	0		12½	1	0		21⅓	1	0		13⅓	1	0		16⅔
1	6		18¾		6		32	1	6		20	1	6		25
2	0		25	2	0		42¾	2	0		26⅔	2	0		33⅓
2	3		28	2	3		48		3		30		3		37½
2	6		31¼	2	6		53½		6		33⅓		6		41⅔
2	9		34⅓		9		58¾		9		36⅔	2	9		45⅚
3	0		37½	3	0		64¼	3	0		40	3	0		50
3	9		46¾	3	9		80⅓		9		50		9		62½
4	0		50	4	0		85⅔	4	0		53⅓	4	0		66⅔
4	6		56¼		6		96⅓	4	6		60		6		75
5	0		62½	5	0	1	7	5	0		66⅔	5	0		83⅓
6	0		75	6	0	1	28½	6	0		80	6	0	1	00
6	9		84⅓	6	9	1	44½		9		90		9	1	12½
7	6		93¾	7	6	1	60⅔	7	6	1	00	7	6	1	25
10	6	1	31¼	10	6	2	25	10	6	1	40	10	6	1	75

Note. In calculating the above table, remainders are not marked, being less than ¼, &c.

£1 of New York and North Carolina, is $2 50
£1 of South Carolina and Georgia, is .. $4 28½ +
£1 of New Jersey, Pennsylvania, Delaware, and Maryland, is $2 66⅔
£1 New Hampshire, Massachusetts, Rhode Island, Connecticut, Virginia, Kentucky, and Tennessee, is . . . $3 33⅓

A TABLE OF COINS, WITH THEIR STERLING AND FEDERAL VALUE.

Names of Coins.	Standard Weight.	Sterling Money of Great Britain.	New Hampshire, Massachusetts, R. Island, Connec'cut, Virginia, Kentucky & Tennessee.	New York, Pennsylvania, and North Carolina.	New Jersey, Pennsylvania, Delaware, and Maryland.	S. Carolina and Georgia.	Federal value.
GOLD.	dwt. gr.	£ s. d.	£ s. d.	£ s. d.	£ s. d.	£ s. d.	$ cts. m.
A Johannes	18 0	3 12 0	4 16 0	6 8 0	6 0 0	4 0 0	16 00 0
A Half Johannes	9 0	1 16 0	2 8 0	3 4 0	3 0 0	2 0 0	8 00 0
A Doubloon	16 21	3 6 0	4 8 0	5 16 0	5 12 6	3 10 0	14 93 3
A Moidore	6 18	1 7 0	1 16 0	2 8 0	2 5 0	1 8 0	6 00 0
An English Guinea	5 6	1 1 0	1 8 0	1 17 0	1 15 0	1 1 9	6 66 7
A French Guinea	5 5	1 1 0	1 7 6	1 16 0	1 14 6	1 1 5	4 60 0
A Spanish Pistole	4 6	0 16 0	1 2 0	1 9 0	1 8 0	0 18 0	3 77 3
A French Pistole	4 4	0 16 0	1 2 0	1 8 0	1 7 6	0 17 6	3 66 7
SILVER.							
An English or French Crown	18 0	0 5 0	0 6 8	0 8 9	0 8 3	0 5 0	1 10 0
The dollar of Spain, Sweden or Denmark	17 6	0 4 6	0 6 0	0 8 0	0 7 6	0 4 8	1 00 0
An English Shilling	3 18	0 1 0	0 1 4	0 1 9	0 1 8	0 1 1	0 22 2
A Pistareen	3 11	0 0 10½	0 1 2	0 1 7	0 1 6	0 0 11	0 20 0

☞ All other gold coins of equal fineness at 86 cents per dwt., and silver at 111 cents per ounce.

A TABLE OF OTHER FOREIGN COINS, &c.,

WITH THEIR VALUE IN FEDERAL MONEY.

	$ cts. m.		cts. m.
Pound Sterling.	4 44 4	The Guilder of the) United Netherlands }	39 0
Pound of Ireland.	4 10 0		
Pagoda of India. .	1 94 0	Mark Banco of) Hamburg }	33 5
Tale of China. .	1 48 0		
Millrea of Portugal.	1 24 0	Livre Tournois of) France }	18 5
Ruble of Russia.	0 66 0		
Rupee of Bengal	55 5	Real Plate of Spain	10 0

Note. Some persons, to try others' skill in numbers, may give them the multiplying of pounds, shillings, pence, &c., by the same; or the multiplying of cents by the same, &c. The following will be sufficient, thus:—Pounds multiplied by pounds, give pounds. Pounds multiplied by shillings, give shillings. Shillings multiplied by shillings, give the 20th part of a shilling. Shillings multiplied by pence, give the 20th part of a penny. Pence multiplied by pence, give the 240th part of a penny, &c.; and cents multiplied by cents, give the 100th part of a cent, &c.

EXCHANGE.

Exchange teaches to change a sum of one kind of money to a given denomination of another kind; to reduce the currency of each of the United States to dollars and cents, or Federal Money.

RULE.

Reduce the sum to pence; to the pence annex two ciphers; then divide by the number of pence which make a dollar in that state or country. The quotient will be cents; which reduce to dollars.

Note. This rule applies to the currency of any state or country, if its currency be in pounds, shillings, pence, &c.

EXAMPLES.

1. In 90 pounds New England, Virginia, Kentucky and

Tennessee currency, how many dollars and cents, a dollar
being 72 pence?

£
90
29
‾‾‾‾
1800
12
‾‾‾‾
72)2160000($300 00
216
‾‾‾‾
0000

2. Bring 12 pounds, 3 shillings and 9 pence to dollars
and cents, same currency.　　　　Ans. $40 62½ cts.
3. Reduce 19 shillings and 10 pence to dollars and cents,
same currency.　　　　Ans. $3 30cts. 5m.
4. In 763 pounds how many dollars, cents and mills,
same currency?　　　　Ans. $2543 33cts. 3m.
5. Reduce 30£ and 3s. to dollars and cents, same currency.　　　　Ans. $100 50 cts.
6. In 27£ 2s. how many dollars and cents, New York
and North Carolina currency, one dollar being 96 pence?
　　　　Ans. $67 75 cts.
7. In 30£ how many dollars and cents, same currency?
　　　　Ans. $75 00 cts.
8. In 9£ 16s. how many dollars and cents, same currency?　　　　Ans. $24 50 cts.
9. In 942£ of New Jersey, Pennsylvania, Delaware and
Maryland currency, how many dollars and cents, a dollar
being 90 pence?　　　　Ans. $2512 00 cts.
10. In 12£ how many dollars and cents, same currency?
　　　　Ans. $32 00 cts.
11. In 86£ 6s. 5d. how many dollars, cents and mills,
same currency?　　　　Ans. $230 18cts. 8m.
12. In 56£, South Carolina and Georgia currency, how
many dollars and cents, being 56 pence in a dollar?
　　　　Ans. $240 00 cts.
13. In 21£ how many dollars and cents, same currency?
　　　　Ans. $90 00 cts.

14. In 460£ and 16s., sterling money, how many dollars and cents, being 54 pence in a dollar? Ans. $2048 00 cts.

To bring dollars, or dollars and cents, to pounds, shillings, &c.

RULE.

Multiply the dollars, or dollars and cents, by the number of pence which make a dollar of the currency into which you wish to bring the given sum. The answer will be pence, which bring to pounds.

Note. If there be cents in the given sum, two figures must be cut off from the right of the product, before bringing them into pounds, &c.

EXAMPLES.

1. In 33 dollars how many pounds, &c. sterling, a dollar being 54 pence?

$$\$$$
$$33$$
$$54$$
$$\overline{}$$
$$132$$
$$165$$
$$\overline{}$$
$$12)1782d.$$
$$\overline{}$$
$$2|0)14|8—6d.$$
$$\overline{}$$

Ans. 7£ 8s. 6d

2. 1,000,000 dollars how many pounds, same currency?
Ans. 225,000£.

3. In 150 dollars 25 cents how many pounds, &c., New England, Virginia, Kentucky and Tennessee currency, a dollar being 72 pence? . Ans. 45£ 1s. 6d.

4. In 2070 dollars, New England, Virginia, Kentucky and Tennessee currency, how many pounds, &c., a dollar being 72 pence? Ans. 621£.

5. In 24 dollars 50 cents how many pounds and shillings, &c., in New York and North Carolina currency, a dollar being 96 cents? A.. 9£ 16s. 0d.

6. In 2512 dollars, how many pounds of New Jersey, Pennsylvania, Delaware, and Maryland currency, a dollar being 90 pence? Ans. 942£.

7. In 90 dollars, how many pounds South Carolina and Georgia currency, a dollar being 56 pence? Ans. 21£.

To change the currency of one state or country into that of another.

RULE.

Place the sum you wish to change, in the third place — the number of shillings in a dollar of that currency into which you wish to change it, in the second — and the number of shillings in a dollar of that currency you wish to change, in the first. Proceed by the Rule of Three.

1. What is the value of 50£ Tennessee currency, in New York?

$$S. \quad S. \quad £.$$
$$6 : 8 :: 50$$
$$8$$

$$6)400$$

Ans. 66£. 13s. 4d.

2. What is the value of 500£ Massachusetts currency, in Pennsylvania? Ans. 625£.

3. What is the value of 100£ South Carolina or Georgia currency, in Kentucky? Ans. 128£. 11s. 5d. +

4. What is the value of 750£ New Hampshire currency, in North Carolina? Ans. 1000£.

VULGAR FRACTIONS.

A Vulgar Fraction is a part of a whole number, and is read by first mentioning the upper part of the fraction, and then the lower, thus: $\frac{1}{4}$, $\frac{5}{8}$, &c. The upper part of the fraction is called the numerator, and shows the part of a whole number expressed by the fraction. The lower number is called the denominator, and shows the number of such parts contained in a whole number. Vulgar Fractions are either proper, improper, compound, or mixed. A proper fraction has its numerator less than its denominator, as $\frac{1}{3}$, $\frac{1}{4}$, &c. An improper fraction has its numerator greater than its denominator, as $\frac{5}{3}$, $\frac{4}{3}$, &c. A compound fraction is a fraction of a fraction, with the word "of" expressed between them, as $\frac{1}{2}$ of $\frac{2}{3}$, of $\frac{1}{4}$, &c. A mixed number is a whole number and a fraction, as $5\frac{1}{2}$, $8\frac{1}{4}$, &c.

REDUCTION OF VULGAR FRACTIONS.

CASE 1.

To reduce a fraction to its lowest terms.

RULE.

Divide the numerator and denominator continually by any number that will divide them both without a remainder. When they cannot be divided by any number without a remainder, the fraction is then at its lowest terms.

EXAMPLES.

1. Reduce $\frac{24}{48}$ to its lowest terms:
$$24)\frac{24}{48} = \frac{1}{2} \text{ Ans.}$$
2. Reduce $\frac{12}{16}$ to its lowest terms. Ans. $\frac{3}{4}$.
3. Reduce $\frac{12}{48}$ to its lowest terms. Ans. $\frac{1}{4}$.
4. Reduce $\frac{192}{324}$ to its lowest terms. Ans. $\frac{3}{4}$.
5. Reduce $\frac{24}{100}$ to its lowest terms. Ans. $\frac{1}{4}$.
6. Reduce $\frac{42}{294}$ to its lowest terms. Ans. $\frac{7}{12}$.

CASE 2.

To reduce a mixed number to an improper fraction.

RULE.

Multiply the whole number by the denominator of the fraction, and add the numerator to the product for a new numerator, under which place the given denominator.

EXAMPLES.

1. Reduce $11\frac{2}{5}$ to an improper fraction. Ans. $\frac{57}{5}$.

$$11\frac{2}{5}$$
$$5$$

New numerator. 57

Denominator. 5

2. Reduce $8\frac{3}{4}$ to an improper fraction.   Ans. $\frac{3\cdot9}{4}$.
3. Reduce $14\frac{1}{2}$ to an improper fraction.   Ans. $\frac{2\cdot9}{2}$.
4. Reduce $99\frac{4}{11}$ to an improper fraction.   Ans. $\frac{10\cdot87}{11}$.

CASE 3.

To reduce an improper fraction to a whole or mixed number.

RULE.

Divide the numerator by the denominator.

EXAMPLES.

1. Reduce $\frac{400}{17}$ to its proper terms.

$$17)400(\text{Ans. } 23\frac{9}{17}.$$
$$34$$
$$\overline{}$$
$$60$$
$$51$$
$$\overline{}$$
$$9$$

2. Reduce $\frac{91}{4}$ to its proper terms.   Ans. $22\frac{3}{4}$
3. Reduce $\frac{51}{10}$ to its proper terms.   Ans. $5\frac{1}{10}$
4. Reduce $\frac{189}{84}$ to its proper terms.   Ans. $2\frac{21}{84}$

Note. Case 2d. and 3rd. prove each other.

CASE 4.

To reduce compound fractions to single ones.

RULE.

Multiply all the numerators together for a new numerator, and all the denominators for a new denominator; which reduce to their lowest terms.

EXAMPLES.

1. Reduce $\frac{1}{2}$ of $\frac{2}{3}$ of $\frac{3}{4}$ of $\frac{4}{5}$ to a single fraction.   Ans. $\frac{1}{5}$.

$$1 \times 2 \times 3 \times 4 = \qquad 24 =$$
$$\qquad\qquad\qquad\qquad 24)\frac{}{}(\frac{1}{5}.$$
$$2 + 3 \times 4 \times 5 = \qquad 120$$

2. Reduce $\frac{2}{3}$ of $\frac{3}{4}$ of $\frac{4}{5}$ to a single fraction.   Ans. $\frac{2}{5}$.

3. Reduce $\frac{4}{5}$ of $\frac{5}{6}$ of $\frac{7}{9}$ to a single fraction.   Ans. $\frac{7}{18}$.

4. Reduce $1\frac{2}{7}$ of $\frac{5}{8}$ of $\frac{1}{2}$ to a single fraction.   Ans. $\frac{5}{11}$.

CASE 5.

To find a common denominator, viz: one whose denominators are all alike.

RULE.

Multiply all the denominators together for a common denominator, into which divide each denominator, and multiply the quotient by its own numerator for a new numerator, and place the new numerator over the common denominator.

EXAMPLES.

1. Reduce $\frac{1}{2}$, $\frac{2}{3}$ and $\frac{3}{4}$ to a common denominator.

$$\begin{array}{ll} \frac{1}{2}\ \frac{2}{3}\ \frac{3}{4} & 12 \times 1 = \ \ 12 \\ \quad\ \ 3 & 8 \times 2 = \ \ 16 \text{ new numerators.} \\ \quad\ - & 6 \times 3 = \ \ 18 \\ \quad\ 12 \\ \quad\ 2 \\ \quad\ - \end{array}$$

Divide by 2, 3, 4. 24 common denominator.

Ans. $\frac{12}{24}$, $\frac{16}{24}$, $\frac{18}{24}$.

2. Reduce $\frac{1}{2}$, $\frac{3}{4}$ and $\frac{7}{8}$ to a common denominator.

Ans. $\frac{32}{64}$, $\frac{48}{64}$, $\frac{56}{64}$.

3. Reduce $\frac{7}{8}$, $\frac{2}{3}$, $\frac{1}{2}$, $\frac{6}{7}$, to a common denominator.

Ans. $\frac{735}{840}$, $\frac{560}{840}$, $\frac{504}{840}$, $\frac{720}{840}$.

4. Reduce $\frac{1}{2}$, $\frac{2}{3}$, $\frac{5}{6}$ and $\frac{7}{8}$, to a common denominator.

Ans. $\frac{144}{288}$, $\frac{192}{288}$, $\frac{240}{288}$, $\frac{252}{288}$.

CASE 6.

To reduce the fraction of one denomination to the fraction of another, but greater, retaining the same value.

RULE.

Make the fraction a compound one, by comparing it with all the denominations between it and that to which it is to be reduced; which fraction reduce to a single one.

EXAMPLES.

1. Reduce $\frac{2}{3}$ of a pennyweight to the fraction of a pound, Troy.

$$\frac{2}{3} \text{ of } \frac{1}{20} \text{ of } \frac{1}{12} \quad 3)\frac{2}{1200} = \frac{1}{400} \text{ Ans.}$$

2. Reduce $\frac{3}{4}$ of a nail to the fraction of a yard.

Ans. $\frac{3}{128}$ yd.

3. Reduce $\frac{5}{9}$ of a cent to the fraction of a dollar.

Ans. $\frac{1}{180}$ dollar.

4. Reduce $\frac{4}{5}$ of a pint to the fraction of a hogshead.

Ans. $\frac{5}{4032}$ hhd.

CASE 7.

To reduce the fraction of one denomination to the fraction of another, but less, retaining the same value.

RULE.

Multiply the given numerator by the parts of the denominator between it and that to which it is reduced, for a new numerator, and place it over the given denominator, which reduce to its lowest terms.

EXAMPLES.

1. Reduce $\frac{1}{180}$ of a dollar to the fraction of a cent.

Ans. $\frac{5}{9}$ cent.

$$\overset{cts.}{\frac{1}{180}} \times \frac{100}{1} = 2|0)\frac{100}{18}|\frac{9}{8} = \frac{5}{9}.$$

2. Reduce $\frac{2}{27}$ of a pound, troy, to the fraction of an ounce.

Ans. $\frac{8}{9}$ oz.

3. Reduce $\frac{2}{252}$ of a cwt. to the fraction of a pound, avoirdupois.

Ans. $\frac{8}{9}$ lb.

4. Reduce $\frac{1}{1587}$ of a day to the fraction of a minute.

Ans. $\frac{10}{11}$ min.

CASE 8.

To reduce a fraction to its proper value.

RULE.

Multiply the numerator by the next lowest denomination, and divide by the denominator.

EXAMPLES.

1. Reduce $\frac{4}{5}$ of a dollar to its proper value.

$$\frac{4}{100}$$

$$5)\overline{400}$$

Ans. 80 cents.

2. Reduce $\frac{3}{4}$ of a dollar to its proper value.
Ans. 75 cents.

3. Reduce $\frac{1}{4}$ of a day to its proper quantity.
Ans. 6 hours.

4. Reduce $\frac{4}{5}$ of a mile to its proper quantity.
Ans. 4fur. 125yd. 2ft. 1in. $\frac{5}{7}$.

5. Reduce $\frac{5}{16}$ of an acre to its proper quantity.
Ans. 1R. 10P.

6. Reduce $\frac{9}{10}$ of a year to its proper quantity.
Ans. 328da. 12hr.

CASE 9.

To reduce any given value, or quantity, to a fraction of any greater denomination of the same kind.

RULE.

Reduce the given sum to the lowest denomination mentioned for a numerator, and the denomination of which you wish to make it a fraction to the same name for a denominator.

EXAMPLES.

1. Reduce 60 cents to the fraction of a dollar.
Ans. $\frac{3}{5}$ dollar.

$$2|0)\tfrac{6}{10}|\tfrac{0}{0} = \tfrac{3}{5}$$

2. Reduce 90 cents to the fraction of a dollar.
Ans. $\frac{9}{10}$ dollar.

3. Reduce 9 ounces, troy, to the fraction of a pound.
Ans. $\frac{3}{4}$ lb.

4. Reduce 9oz. 2dr. $\frac{2}{7}$, avoirdupois, to the fraction of a pound.
Ans. $\frac{4}{7}$ lb.

5. Reduce 3qr. 3na. to the fraction of a yard. Ans. $\frac{15}{16}$.

6. Reduce 7 months to the fraction of a year.
Ans. $\frac{7}{12}$ year.

ADDITION OF VULGAR FRACTIONS.

RULE.

Reduce the fractions to a common denominator; then add all the numerators together, and place their sum over the common denominator. If fractions be of different denominations, find their value separately, and add as in Compound Addition.

Note. If mixed numbers be given, reduce them to improper fractions, or only use the fractional part in performing the operation. Then add the whole numbers, as in Simple Addition. If compound fractions be given, reduce them to single ones.

EXAMPLES.

1. Add $\frac{1}{8}$, $\frac{1}{2}$, and $\frac{1}{4}$, together. Ans. $\frac{7}{8}$.

$$\frac{1}{8} \quad \frac{1}{2} \quad \frac{1}{4} \qquad 8 \qquad 8)\frac{1\,2\,4}{6\,4} = \frac{7}{8}$$
$$2 \qquad 32$$
$$\overline{8} \qquad 16$$
$$8 \qquad \frac{5\,2}{6\,4}$$

Divide by 8, 2, 4)$\overline{64}$

2. Add $\frac{2}{5}$ and $\frac{5}{10}$, together. Ans. $\frac{9}{10}$.
3. Add $\frac{3}{4}$, $\frac{1}{7}$, $\frac{9}{10}$, and $\frac{2}{3}$, together. Ans. $3\frac{23}{120}$.
4. Add $\frac{7}{11}$, $\frac{3}{11}$, $\frac{3}{11}$, and $\frac{4}{11}$, together. Ans. $\frac{19}{11}$.
5. Add $\frac{1}{8}$, $\frac{1}{2}$, and $\frac{1}{4}$, together. Ans. $1\frac{1}{2}$.
6. Add $3\frac{1}{4}$, $8\frac{2}{7}$, and $\frac{4}{9}$, together. Ans. $11\frac{247}{252}$.
7. Add $7\frac{2}{7}$, and $5\frac{4}{5}$, together. Ans. $13\frac{8}{35}$.
8. Add $\frac{1}{3}$ of an acre to $\frac{7}{10}$ of a rood. Ans. 2R. $1\frac{1}{3}$P.
9. Add $\frac{3}{4}$ of a mile to $\frac{7}{10}$ of a furlong. Ans. 6fur. 28P.
10. Add $\frac{3}{6}$ of $\frac{5}{8}$ and $\frac{1}{6}$ of $\frac{7}{12}$ together. Ans. $\frac{29}{48}$.
11. Add $\frac{1}{3}$ of $\frac{1}{7}$ and $\frac{3}{8}$ of $\frac{12}{28}$ together. Ans. $\frac{3}{47}$.

MULTIPLICATION OF VULGAR FRACTIONS.

RULE.

Multiply the numerators together for a new numerator, and the denominators for a new denominator.

Note. If compound fractions be given, reduce them to single ones; or, if mixed numbers, reduce them to improper fractions; and proceed as before.

EXAMPLES.

1. Multiply $\frac{1}{2}$ by $\frac{2}{3}$, $\frac{1}{2} \times \frac{2}{3} = \frac{2}{6}$ 2)$\frac{2}{6}$.　　Ans. $\frac{1}{6}$.
2. Multiply $\frac{1}{7}$ by $\frac{1}{2}$.　　Ans. $\frac{7}{10}$.
3. Multiply $\frac{2}{16}$ by $\frac{1}{3}$.　　Ans. $\frac{1}{14}$.
4. Multiply $4\frac{1}{2}$ by $\frac{2}{3}$.　　Ans. $3\frac{1}{2}$.
5. Multiply $\frac{1}{3}$ of $\frac{4}{1}$ by $\frac{7}{10}$ of $1\frac{1}{2}$.　　Ans. $\frac{77}{480}$.
6. Multiply $\frac{1}{2}$ of 7 by $\frac{1}{2}$.　　Ans. $1\frac{3}{4}$.

$$\frac{1}{2} \times \frac{7}{1} \times \frac{1}{2} = \frac{7}{4} \qquad 4)7$$

$$1\frac{3}{4}.$$

SUBTRACTION OF VULGAR FRACTIONS.

RULE.

Reduce compound fractions to single ones, and mixed numbers to improper fractions. Then reduce these fractions to a common denominator, and subtract the less numerator from the greater, and place the difference over the common denominator.

Note. When the fractions are of different denominations, reduce them to their proper value, each separately, and take their difference by Compound Subtraction.

EXAMPLES.

1. From $\frac{6}{8}$ take $\frac{5}{12}$.　　Ans. $\frac{5}{24}$.

$$8$$

$$12 \times 5 = 60$$

Divide by 8, 12)96　　$8 \times 5 = 40$

$$4)\frac{20}{48} = \frac{5}{24}.$$

2. From $\frac{7}{8}$ take $\frac{4}{5}$.　　Ans. $\frac{3}{40}$.
3. From $\frac{9}{10}$ take $\frac{5}{16}$.　　Ans. $\frac{2}{5}$.
4. From $\frac{7}{15}$ take $\frac{9}{20}$.　　Ans. $\frac{1}{60}$.
5. From $\frac{1}{2}$ of $\frac{2}{3}$ take $\frac{2}{3}$ of $\frac{4}{5}$.　　Ans. $\frac{1}{6}$.
6. From $\frac{2}{3}$ of $\frac{7}{15}$ take $\frac{1}{4}$ of $\frac{3}{8}$.　　Ans. $\frac{17}{120}$.
7. From $\frac{1}{2}$ of a league take $\frac{7}{10}$ of a mile.

Ans. 1m. 2fur. 16p.

8. From $\frac{7}{8}$ of a yard take $\frac{3}{4}$ of an inch.   Ans. $5\frac{1}{4}$ in

Note. When fractions or mixed numbers are to be subtracted from whole numbers, subtract the numerator of the fraction from its denominator, and under the remainder place the denominator; then carry one, to be subtracted from the whole number.

9. From 5 take $\frac{9}{14}$.   Ans. $4\frac{5}{14}$.

$$\begin{array}{cc} 5 & \frac{9}{14} \\ 1 & 8 \\ \hline 4 & \frac{6}{14} \end{array}$$

10. From 10 take $\frac{1}{10}$.   Ans. $9\frac{9}{10}$.
11. From 9 take $5\frac{1}{2}$.   Ans. $3\frac{1}{2}$.
12. From 25 take $24\frac{8}{10}$.   Ans. $\frac{1}{5}$.

DIVISION OF VULGAR FRACTIONS.

RULE.

Reduce compound fractions to single ones, and mixed numbers to improper fractions. Then invert the dividing term, and multiply all the numerators into each other for a dividend, and denominators for a divisor.

EXAMPLES.

1. Divide $\frac{1}{2}$ by $\frac{3}{4}$.   Ans. $\frac{2}{3}$.
     inverted $\frac{4}{3} \times \frac{1}{2}$ 2)$\frac{4}{6} = \frac{2}{3}$.
2. Divide 6 by $\frac{1}{8}$.   Ans. 48.
3. Divide $\frac{5}{9}$ by 3.   Ans. $\frac{5}{27}$.
4. Divide $\frac{17}{21}$ by $\frac{3}{5}$.   Ans. $1\frac{22}{63}$.
5. Divide $6\frac{3}{5}$ by $\frac{1}{3}$.   Ans. $19\frac{4}{5}$.
6. Divide $\frac{2}{3}$ of $\frac{1}{4}$ by $\frac{1}{2}$ of $\frac{3}{4}$.   Ans. $\frac{20}{27}$.
7. Divide $\frac{2}{3}$ of $\frac{3}{4}$ by $\frac{1}{2}$ of $\frac{2}{3}$.   Ans. $1\frac{1}{2}$.
8. Divide $\frac{2}{3}$ of $\frac{7}{8}$ by $\frac{1}{4}$ of $\frac{1}{7}$.   Ans. $16\frac{1}{3}$.
9. Divide $4\frac{1}{5}$ by $\frac{4}{5}$ of 4.   Ans. $2\frac{1}{20}$.
10. What part of $33\frac{1}{21}$ is $28\frac{11}{12}$?   Ans. $\frac{7}{8}$.

RULE OF THREE, IN VULGAR FRACTIONS.

RULE.

State as in whole numbers. Then invert the first term, and multiply all the numerators together for a dividend, and denominators for a divisor. If mixed numbers be given, reduce them to improper fractions; or compound fractions to single ones. If a whole number, place it thus: $\frac{6}{1}, \frac{7}{1}$, &c.

EXAMPLES.

1. If $\frac{2}{5}$ of a yard of cloth cost $\frac{4}{5}$ of a dollar, how much will $\frac{4}{5}$ of a yard cost at that rate?   Ans. $1 60 cts.

$$\text{Inverted } \tfrac{5}{2} \times \tfrac{4}{5} \times \tfrac{4}{5} \times 5\text{)}8\text{)}0$$

$$\overline{\quad\quad}$$

$$\$1\ 60 \text{ cts.}$$

2. If $\frac{3}{4}$ of an ounce of indigo cost $\frac{1}{4}$ of a dollar, how much will $\frac{5}{8}$ of an ounce cost?   Ans. $23\frac{7}{16}$ cts.

3. If $1\frac{1}{4}$ bushels of corn cost $1\frac{1}{4}$, how much will 60 bushels cost at that rate?   Ans. $38 $57\frac{1}{4}$ cts.

4. If $2\frac{1}{2}$ bushels oats cost 50 cents, what cost $13\frac{1}{4}$ bushels at that rate?   Ans. $2 65 cts.

5. How many yards of linen, $\frac{5}{4}$ wide, will be sufficient to line 20 yards of baize, that is $\frac{3}{4}$ of a yard wide?   Ans. 12 yd.

6. If $\frac{1}{3}$ of a pound of cinnamon bring $\frac{4}{7}$ of a dollar, what will $1\frac{3}{5}$ lb. come to?   Ans. $2 $74\frac{2}{7}$ cts.

7. What will $\frac{1}{8}$ of $2\frac{1}{2}$ cwt. of chocolate come to, when $6\frac{1}{2}$ lb. cost $\frac{3}{4}$ of a dollar?   Ans. $10 $76\frac{12}{13}$ cts.

8. When 10 men can finish a piece of work in $20\frac{2}{3}$ days, in how many days can 6 men do the same?   Ans. $34\frac{4}{9}$ da.

9. How many pieces of stuff, at $20\frac{1}{4}$ per piece, are equal in value to $240\frac{1}{7}$ pieces, at $12\frac{1}{2}$ per piece?   Ans. $149\frac{177}{1127}$.

10. If $\frac{1}{2}$ of $\frac{2}{3}$ of $\frac{3}{4}$ of 60 cents will pay for a bushel of potatoes, how many bushel will $1 60 cts. pay for?   Ans. $10\frac{2}{3}$ bu.

DOUBLE RULE OF THREE IN VULGAR FRACTIONS.

RULE.

Prepare the terms, if necessary, by Reduction. State as in whole numbers. Then invert the two dividing terms, and multiply all numerators together for a dividend, and the denominators for a divisor.

EXAMPLES.

1. If $\frac{1}{2}$ of a dollar, in $\frac{9}{12}$ of a year, gain $\frac{1}{25}$ of a dollar interest, how much will $\frac{5}{8}$ of a dollar gain in $\frac{5}{6}$ of a year?

Ans. $5\frac{5}{9}$ cts.

$$\text{Principal.} \quad \begin{matrix} \$ & y. & \$ \\ \frac{1}{2} : \frac{9}{12} :: \frac{1}{25} \text{ Interest.} \\ \frac{5}{8} : \frac{5}{6} \end{matrix}$$

$$\text{Inverted } \frac{2}{1} \times \frac{12}{9} \times \frac{5}{8} \times \frac{5}{6} \times \frac{1}{25} = 108|00)600|00 = 5\frac{5}{9}.$$
$$540$$
$$\overline{\quad 60\quad}$$

2. If $2\frac{1}{4}$ yards of cloth, $1\frac{1}{2}$ yards wide, cost $\$3\frac{3}{4}$, what is the value of $38\frac{1}{4}$ yards, 2 yards wide?   Ans. $\$76$ 50 cts.

3. If $\$50$ in $4\frac{1}{30}$ months gain $2\frac{1}{4}$ dollars interest, in what time will $\$15\frac{1}{5}$ gain $\$2$?   Ans. $12\frac{472}{477}$ months.

4. If 4 men in $5\frac{1}{4}$ days eat $7\frac{1}{2}$ lb. of bread, how many pounds will 20 men eat in $\frac{5}{8}$ of a day?   Ans. $5\frac{45}{116}$ lb.

5. If 90 dollars in $\frac{1}{3}$ of a year gain $\$4\frac{1}{2}$ interest, in what time will 900 dollars gain 20 dollars interest?

Ans. $4\frac{4}{35}$ months.

DECIMAL FRACTIONS.

A Decimal Fraction is a part of a whole number or unit, denoted by a point placed to the left of a figure or figures; as .2, .18, .110. The first figure after the point denotes so many tenths of a unit; the second, so many hundredths; the third, so many thousandths; and so on.

Decimal Fractions are read in the same manner as vulgar fractions. .5 is equal to, and reads as $\frac{5}{10}$, $.10\frac{10}{100}$, $.120\frac{120}{1000}$, and so on. A mixed number consisting of a whole number and a decimal, as $12\frac{5}{10}$; thus 12.5. Whole numbers, counting from the right towards the left, increase in a ten-fold proportion; but decimals, counting from the left towards the right, decrease in a tenfold proportion, as will be better exemplified in the following table:

TABLE.

100 of Millions.	10 of Millions.	Millions.	100 of Thousands.	10 of Thousands.	Thousands.	Hundreds.	Tens.	Units.		Tenth part.	Hundredth part.	Thousandth part.	10 Thousandth part.	100 Thousandth part.	Millionth part.	10 Millionth part.	100 Millionth part.	1000 Millionth part.
2	2	2	2	2	2	2	2	1		1	2	2	2	2	2	2	2	2

Whole numbers.　　　　　Decimals.

Note. Ciphers annexed to decimals, neither increase or decrease them; thus, .4, .10, .50, being $\frac{4}{10}$, $\frac{10}{100}$, $\frac{50}{100}$, are of the same value; but ciphers prefixed to decimals, decrease them in a tenfold proportion; thus, .04, .010, .050, being $\frac{4}{100}$, $\frac{10}{1000}$, $\frac{50}{1000}$, &c.

ADDITION OF DECIMALS.

RULE.

Write down the given numbers under each other, viz. :—Units under units, tens under tens, &c., and add as in addition of whole numbers; observing to set the point in the answer under those of the given number.

EXAMPLES.

(1.) 2.12	(2.) 36.12	(3.) .7324
.103	3.112	.0962
15.115	.12	.132
.74	16.182	.09
18.078	55.534	1.0506

4. Add 56.12, .7, 1.314, 5837.01, and .15, together.
　　　　　　　　　　　　　　　　　Ans. 5895.294.

5. Add 361.04, .120, 78.0006, 101.54, 8.943, and .3, together.　　　　　　　　　　　　　Ans. 549.9436.

MULTIPLICATION OF DECIMALS.

RULE.

Multiply as in whole numbers, and point off as many figures in the product for decimals as there are decimals in both factors. If there are not so many figures in the product as there are decimal figures in both factors, place ciphers to the left of the product to supply the deficiency.

EXAMPLES.

1. Multiply 5.11 by .122

```
      5.11

       122
       122
       610
      _____
     .62342
```

2. Multiply 54.20 by 38.63.   Ans. 2093.7460.
3. Multiply 4560. by .3720.   Ans. 1696.3200.
4. Multiply .285 by .003.   Ans. .000855.
5. Multiply 3.92 by 196.   Ans. 768.32
6. Multiply .28043 by .0005.   Ans. .000140215.

SUBTRACTION OF DECIMALS.

RULE.

Place the numbers as in addition, with the less under the greater; and subtract as in whole numbers, setting the point in the answer under those in the given numbers.

EXAMPLES.

1. From 32.456 take 1.33

```
      1.33

Ans. 31.126
```

2. From 18.16 take 9.125.   Ans. 9.035
3. From 100. take .25.   Ans. 99.75

4. From 441.2 take 128.9   Ans. 312.3.
5. From 456.1 take 111.9   Ans. 344.2.

DIVISION OF DECIMALS.

RULE.

Divide as in whole numbers; then observe how many more decimal figures there are in the dividend than divisor, and point off that number of decimal figures in the answer. Or if there be not figures enough in the answer, annex ciphers until there be a sufficient number.

Note. If the dividend be not large enough to contain the divisor, annex ciphers until it will be; or if there be a remainder, proceed in like manner.

EXAMPLES.

1. Divide 148.63 by 4.21

$$4.21)148.63(\text{Ans. } 35.3040$$
$$126.3$$

$$2233$$
$$2105$$

$$128.0$$
$$126.3$$

$$17.00$$
$$16.84$$

$$160$$

2. Divide 19.25 by 38.5   Ans. .5.
3. Divide .2142 by 3.2   Ans. .066. +
4. Divide 210. by 240.   Ans. .875.
5. Divide .1606 by 4.4   Ans. .865.
6. Divide 3. by 4.   Ans. .75.
7. Divide 275. by 3842.   Ans. .071577. +

REDUCTION OF DECIMALS.

CASE 1.

To reduce a vulgar fraction to a decimal.

RULE.

Annex ciphers to the numerator, and divide by the denominator. If compound fractions be given, reduce them to single ones, and then to a decimal.

EXAMPLES.

1. Reduce $\frac{1}{2}$ to a decimal. $\frac{1}{2}$ Ans. .5.

$$2)1.0$$
$$\overline{\hphantom{2)}5}$$

2. Reduce $\frac{1}{3}$ to a decimal.   Ans. .333
3. Reduce $\frac{3}{4}$ to a decimal.   Ans. .75
4. Reduce $\frac{3}{8}$ to a decimal.   Ans. .375.
5. Reduce $\frac{1}{2}$ of $\frac{3}{3}$ to a decimal.   Ans. .333. +

CASE 2.

To reduce any sum or quantity to the decimal of a higher.

RULE.

Reduce the given sum to the lowest denomination mentioned for a dividend, and one of that denomination of which you wish to make a decimal to the same denomination for a divisor. The quotient will be the answer.

EXAMPLES.

1. Reduce 2qr. to the decimal of a yard.   Ans. .5

$$
\begin{array}{c}
yd. \\
1 \\
4 \\
\hline
4
\end{array}
\qquad
\begin{array}{c}
4)20 \\
\hline
5
\end{array}
$$

2. Reduce 2qr. 2na. to the decimal of a yard.

     Ans. .625.

3. Reduce 2qt. 1pt. to the decimal of a hhd.

     Ans. .00992 +

4. Reduce 10gr. to the decimal of an ounce, apothecaries' weight.   Ans. .02083. +

5. Reduce 5 minutes to the decimal of an hour.
                 Ans. .08333. +

6. Reduce 2r. 4p. to the decimal of an acre.   Ans. .525.

CASE 3.

To reduce a decimal fraction to its proper value.

RULE.

Multiply the given fraction continually by the next lowest denomination than that of the given sum, for the proper value.

EXAMPLES.

1. What is the value of .75 of a dollar?   Ans. 75cts.

$$- \ 100$$

$$\overline{75.00}$$

2. What is the value of .375 of a dollar?   Ans. 37½cts.

3. What is the value of .9 of an acre?   Ans. 3r. 23p.

4. What is the value of .436 of a yard?
             Ans. 1qr. 2na. .976.

5. What is the value of .71 of 4 ounces, troy?
             Ans. 2oz. 16dwt. 19.2gr.

6. What is the value of .86 of cwt.?
             Ans. 3qr. 12lb. 5oz. 1.92dr.

7. What is the value of .07 of a barrel of 32 gallons?
             Ans. 2gal. 1.92pt.

8. What is the value of .235 of a day?
             Ans. 5hr. 38min. 24sec.

RULE OF THREE IN DECIMALS.

RULE.

State as in whole numbers, only observing when you multiply and divide, to place the decimal points according to the rules of multiplication and division of decimals.

EXAMPLES.

1. If 6.4 lb. of coffee cost 1.22 dollars, what cost 25.6 lb. 6.4 : 25.6 : : 1.22 ?   Ans. $4 88 cents.

2. If 1.4 lb. of sugar cost .16 of a dollar, what will 30cwt. 1qr. 22.5 lb. come to ?   Ans. $389.771. +

3. If I sell 1qr. of cloth for $2.345, what is it per yard ?   Ans. $9.38.

4. How many pieces of cloth at $20.8 per piece are equal in value to 240 pieces at $12.6 per piece ?   Ans. 145.38. +

5. How long will 3 men be in performing a piece of work which will occupy 5 men for 40.5 days?   Ans. 67.5 days.

6. How much muslin .75 of a yard wide will line 25.5 yards of cloth that is 5 quarters wide?   Ans. 42.5 yards.

INVOLUTION; OR, RAISING OF POWERS.

A power is the product produced by multiplying any given number into itself a certain number of times.

Thus, $3 \times 3 = 9$, the square or second power.
$3 \times 3 \times 3 = 27$, the cube or third power of 3.
$3 \times 3 \times 3 \times 3 \times = 81$, the fourth power of three, &c

The number which denotes a power is called its index. Any number multiplied by the same sum one time, the product is its square. Thus, 2 by $\times 2 = 4$, the square of 2, &c. Any number multiplied into its square, the product will be the cube. Thus, $2 \times 2 \times 2 = 8$, the cube of 2. When any power of a vulgar fraction is required, first raise the numerator to the required power for a new numerator, and then raise the denominator to the required power for a new denominator. Thus, the third power of $\frac{2}{3} \times \frac{2}{3} \times \frac{2}{3} =$.
         Ans. $\frac{8}{7}$ the required powers.

TABLE OF THE FIRST NINE POWERS.

Roots.	Squares.	Cubes.	4th Power.	5th Power.	6th Power.	7th Power.	8th Power.	9th Power.
1	1	1	1	1	1	1	1	1
2	4	8	16	32	64	128	256	512
3	9	27	81	243	729	2187	6561	19683
4	16	64	256	1024	4096	16384	65536	262144
5	25	125	625	3125	15625	78125	390625	1953125
6	36	216	1296	7776	46656	279936	1679616	10077696
7	49	343	2401	16807	117649	823543	5764801	40353607
8	64	512	4096	32768	262144	2097152	16777216	134217728
9	81	729	6561	59049	531441	4782969	43046721	387420489

EXAMPLES.

1. What is the square of 8 ?   Ans. 64.
2. What is the square of 9 ?   Ans. 81.
3. What is the cube of 4 ?   Ans. 64.
4. What is the cube of 5 ?   Ans. 125.
5. What is the cube or third power of .263 ?
                                      Ans. .018191447.
6. What is the 6th power of 2.8 ?   Ans. 481.890304.
7. What is the 8th power of $\frac{1}{4}$?   Ans. $\frac{1}{65536}$.

The root of a number is that which will produce that number by being multiplied by itself a given number of times; thus, 2 is the square root of 4, because twice 2 make 4; and 4 is the cube root of 64, because $4 \times 4 \times 4 =$ make 64; and so on.

SQUARE ROOT.

When the square root of any given number is required.

RULE.

Separate the given number into periods of two figures each, beginning at the units' place, find the greatest square contained in the left hand period, and set its root on the right of the given number. Subtract said square from the left hand period, and to the remainder bring down the next period for a dividend. 2d. Double the root for a divisor, and try how often this divisor is contained in the dividend, omitting the last figure, and place the result to the right of the ascertained root; and to the right of the number produced by doubling the ascertained root. Multiply and subtract as in division; and bring down the next period to the remainder for a dividend. Double the ascertained root for a divisor, and proceed as before, till all the periods are brought down.

Note. If the square root of a whole number and decimal are required, point the whole number from right to left; then begin with the decimal, and point from left to right; if there be only one figure at the last, place a cipher to its right to make an even period.

EXAMPLES.

1. What is the square root of 451584?

$$45.15.84(\text{Ans. } 672 \text{ root.}$$
$$36$$

$$127)915$$
$$889$$

$$1342)2684$$
$$2684$$

2. What is the square root of 106929?   Ans. 327.
3. What is the square root of 6.9169?   Ans. 2.63.
4. What is the square root of 393756?   Ans. 627. +
5. What is the square root of 10.4976?   Ans. 3.24.
6. What is the square root of 18.3621?   Ans. 4.28. +
7. What is the square root of 160000?   Ans. 400.
8. What is the square root of .250000?   Ans. .500.
9. What is the square root of 5?   Ans. 2.23. +

Note. When the square root of a vulgar fraction is required, extract the square root of the numerator for a new

numerator, and the square root of the denominator for a
new denominator. If there be a remainder, either to the
numerator or denominator, reduce the fraction to a decimal,
and extract the square root thereof; or if there be a mixed
number, reduce it to an improper fraction, and proceed as
before.

10. What is the square root of $\frac{1444}{1764}$? . Ans. $\frac{4}{5}$.
11. What is the square root of $\frac{2449}{3266}$? . Ans. $\frac{7}{8}$.
12. What is the square root of $\frac{2704}{4423}$? Ans. $\frac{4}{5}$.
13. What is the square root of $\frac{328}{800}$? Ans. $\frac{4}{5}$.
14. What is the square root of $27\frac{9}{16}$? Ans. $5\frac{1}{4}$.
15. What is the square root of $30\frac{1}{4}$? Ans. $5\frac{5}{10}$.

16. A certain young man gave 484 apples to a number
of girls, each girl received as many apples as there were
girls; how many girls were there? Ans. 22.

17. A person being desirous to lay off 3 acres, 2 roods,
5 poles of land, in such a manner as to form a square field,
what must be the length of one of its squares?

Ans. 23.76 poles. +

18. The square of a certain number is 124600, what is
that number? Ans. 352. +

Note. To find the longest side of a right angled triangle.
Square each number, and extract the square root of their
sum. If the shortest side be required, extract the square
root of their difference.

19. Suppose two men depart from Baltimore; one of them
travels due east 90 miles; the other due north 40 miles;
how far are they asunder? Ans. 98.48 miles. +

20. Suppose a wall be 20 feet high, and be surrounded
by a creek 50 feet wide; how long must a line be to reach
from the top of the wall to the opposite bank of the creek?

Ans. 53.85 feet. +

21. Said James to Joseph, I see a tree known to be 100
feet high, and from the spot where I stand it is 40 feet to
its root, but I demand the distance from where I stand to
its top? Ans. 107.70 feet.

22. A certain castle which is 45 feet high, is surrounded

by a ditch 60 feet broad. What length must a ladder be to reach from the outside of the ditch to the top of the castle?   Ans. 75 feet.

23. What is the height of a steeple, when a line 204 feet long will reach from the top of the steeple to the opposite bank of a river, known to be 41 feet broad?
Ans. 199.83 feet. +

24. A certain general has an army of 5625 men; how many must he place in rank and file to form them into a square?   Ans. 75 men.

25. Suppose a ladder, 60 feet long, be so planted as to reach a window 37 feet from the ground on one side of the street, and without moving it at the foot will reach a window 23 feet high on the other side. What is the breadth of the street?   Ans. 102.64 feet

---

CUBE ROOT

When the cube root of any number is required.

RULE.

1st. Separate the given number into periods of three figures, each beginning at the units' place. 2nd. Find the greatest cube contained in the left hand period, and set its root on the right of the given number. 3rd. Subtract said cube from the left hand period; bring down the next period to the remainder for a dividend. 4th. Square the root and multiply the square by 3 for a defective divisor. 5th. Try how often the defective divisor is contained in the dividend, omitting the two right hand figures, and place the number of times it is contained to the right of the ascertained root, and its square to the right of the defective divisor, supplying the place of tens with a cipher, if the square be less than 10. 6th. Multiply the last figure of the root by all the figures in it previously ascertained; multiply that product by 30; and add their products to the divisor to complete it. 7th. Multiply and subtract, as in Division. 8th. And to the remainder bring down the next period for a new dividend. 9th. Find a divisor as before: and thus proceed until all the periods are brought down.

Note. When remainders occur, annex ciphers for decimal periods; and point decimals as in the Square Root.

EXAMPLES.

1. What is the cube root of 10793861?   Ans. 221.

$$10.793.861(221. \cdot$$
$$8$$

Defective divisor and square of 2 = 1204)2793
+ 120 = complete divisor   1324)2648

Defective divisor and square of 1 = 145201)145.861
+ 660 = complete divisor   145861)145.861

2. What is the cube root of 16194277?   Ans. 253.
3. What is the cube root of 5735339?   Ans. 179.
4. What is the cube root of 7532641?   Ans. 196. +
5. What is the cube root of 12.113847?   Ans. 2.29. +
6. What is the cube root of .378621?   Ans. .72. +

Note. When the cube root of a vulgar fraction is required, reduce it to its lowest terms, and extract the cube root of the numerator and of the denominator. If there be a remainder to the numerator or denominator, reduce the fraction to a decimal, and extract the cube root thereof. When mixed numbers are given, reduce them to improper fractions, or to a decimal, and proceed as before.

7. What is the cube root of $\frac{343}{680}$?   Ans. $\frac{5}{7}$.
8. What is the cube root of $\frac{648}{3000}$?   Ans. $\frac{3}{5}$.
9. What is the cube root of $\frac{29}{36}$?   Ans. 3.32. +
10. There has been a cellar dug, out of which has been taken 3456 cubical feet; what is the length, breadth, and depth of it?   Ans. 15ft. +

SINGLE POSITION

Single position is used when it is required to make use of only one supposed number to find an unknown number.

RULE.

Suppose any number most suitable, and proceed with it

as if it were the true one; setting down the result, which is the first term; the given number the second; the supposed number the third. Proceed by Rule of Three. The quotient will be the number sought.

1. A person having about him a certain number of dollars, said, if a $\frac{1}{3}$, a $\frac{1}{4}$, and a $\frac{1}{6}$, were added together, the sum would be 90; how many had he?

$$
\begin{array}{c|l}
\frac{1}{3} & 12 \text{ (Supposed.)} \\
\hline
\frac{1}{4} & 4 \\
\frac{1}{6} & 3 \\
& 2
\end{array}
\qquad
\begin{array}{c|l}
3 & 120 \\
4 & \\
6 & 40 \\
\hline
& 30 \\
& 20
\end{array}
$$

9 : 90 : : 12 (Ans. $120. $90 proof.

2. A merchant received a number of dollars, said $\frac{1}{3}$, $\frac{1}{4}$, $\frac{1}{3}$, and $\frac{1}{5}$ of the number is 90; what number of dollars has he? Ans. 75.

3. A. and B. having found a purse of money, disputed who should have it; A. said that $\frac{1}{5}$, $\frac{1}{10}$, and $\frac{1}{20}$ of it amounted to 35 dollars, and if B. could tell him how much was in it he should have the whole, otherwise he should have nothing; how much did the purse contain? Ans. $100.

4. A person after spending $\frac{1}{2}$ and $\frac{1}{8}$ of his money, had 26$\frac{2}{3}$ dollars left, how much had he at first? Ans. $160.

5. A certain sum of money is to be divided among 5 men, in such a manner that A. shall have $\frac{1}{4}$, B. $\frac{1}{8}$, C. $\frac{1}{10}$, D. $\frac{1}{20}$, and E. the remainder, which is 40 dollars; what is the sum? Ans. $100.

6. A gentleman being asked his age, replied: if the years of my life were doubled, and $\frac{3}{5}$ of the product divided by 3, the result would be 14; what was his age? Ans. 35 years.

7. In a certain web of cloth there is $\frac{1}{2}$ blue, $\frac{1}{3}$ black, and 9 yards white, how many yards are there in the web? Ans. 54 yards.

8. A youth who was desirous to know the age of a fair Miss, to whom he had made his addresses, was replied to in the following manner: If you multiply the years of my life by 3, $\frac{3}{4}$ of the product will be three times the square root of 16. What was her age? Ans. 14 years.

DOUBLE POSITION.

Double Position teaches to find the true number by making use of two supposed numbers.

RULE.

Suppose two numbers most suitable, and work with each according to the nature of the question, observing the errors of the result. Multiply the errors of each operation into the contrary supposed number. If the errors be alike, i. e., both too much or both too little, take their difference for a divisor, and the difference of the products for a dividend; but if the errors be unlike, that is, one too great, and the other too small, take their sum for a divisor, and the sum of the products for a dividend. Proof as in Single Position.

EXAMPLES.

1. A. B. and C. would divide $100 among them, so as that A. may have 5 more than B., and B. 10 more than C. The share of each is required.

```
Suppose      A. 50    Again suppose A. 45
             B. 45                  B. 40
             C. 35                  C. 30
             ---                    ---
             130                    115
             100                    100
             ---                    ---
             30 error too much.     15 error too much.
2d supposed No. 45                  50 1st suppos'd No.
             ---                    ---
             150                    750
             120
             ---
error 30    1350
error 15     750
   --        ---
difference 15 15)600(
                600
                ---
                  0
```

Ans. { A. 40
       B. 35.
       C. 25

Proof 100.

2. A laborer engaged himself for 50 days upon these conditions: that for every day he worked he should receive one dollar; and that for every day he was idle he should forfeit 50 cents. At settlement, he received $27 50 cents. How many days did he work, and how many was he idle?

Ans. Worked 35, idle 15 days.

3. Bought cloth for a coat at $6 per yard, and linen to line it at $1 per yard. The number of yards was 12, and the whole cost $42; how many yards were there of each?

Ans. 6 yards each.

4. A farmer having driven his cattle to market, received for them all, $320; being paid at the rate of $24 per ox, $16 per cow, and $6 per calf. There were as many oxen as cows, and four times as many calves; how many were there of each? Ans. 5 oxen, 5 cows, and 20 calves.

5. A man, when driving sheep to market, was asked where he was going with his score of sheep? who answered he had no score; but if he had as many more, half as many more, and two sheep and a half, he would have a score. How many had he? Ans. 7 sheep.

ALLIGATION

Alligation is a rule for mixing simples of different qualities in such a manner that the composition may be of a middle quality. When the quantity and rates of the simples are given to find the rate of mixture, compounded of their simples.

RULE.

Find the value of each quantity, according to their respective costs; then divide their whole value by the sum of the several quantities.

EXAMPLES.

1. If 4 pounds, at 20 cents per pound, 6 pounds, at 25 cents, and 8 pounds, at 30 cents per pound, be mixed together, what will a pound of the mixture be worth?

11

```
lb.   cts.
 4 at 20 =   80
 6 at 25 =  150
 8 at 30 =  240
 ――          18)470(Ans. 26 cents. +
 18           36
              ――
             110
             108
             ――
               2
```

2. If a person have 4 lb. of tea, at 90 cents per lb., 8 lb. at 75 cents per lb., and 6 lb. at 110 cents per lb., to mix together, what will a pound of the mixture be worth?

Ans. 90 cents.

3. If 4oz. of silver, worth 75 cents per ounce, be melted with 8oz., worth 60 cents per ounce, what will 1oz. of the mixture be worth?

Ans. 65 cents.

4. A farmer mingled 20 bushels of wheat, at 50 cents per bushel, 36 bushels of rye, at 40 cents per bushel, with 30 bushels of corn, at 20 cents per bushel, what is the worth of one bushel of the mixture?

Ans. 35¼ cents. +

5. A grocer has 2cwt. of coffee, at $25 per cwt., 4cwt. at $20 50 cents per cwt, and 7cwt. at $18 62½ cents per cwt., which he will mix together; what will 1cwt. of this mixture be worth?

Ans. $20 18½ cents.

ARITHMETICAL PROGRESSION.

Any rank or series of numbers increasing or decreasing, is by a common difference in Arithmetical Progression, as 1, 2, 3, 4, 5, 6; — 6, 5, 4, 3, 2, 1; — 1, 3, 5, 7, 9, 11; — 11, 9, 7, 5, 3, 1. There are five things to be particularly attended to in Arithmetical Progression, the first and last terms; the number of terms; the common difference, and the sum of all the terms.

CASE 1.

The first term, common difference, and number of terms being given, to find the last term and sum of all the terms.

RULE.

Multiply the number of terms less one, by the common difference; to that product add the first term; the sum is the last term. Add the first and last terms together, and multiply their sum by the number of terms, and half the product will be the sum of all the terms.

EXAMPLES.

1. What is the last term and sum of all the terms of an Arithmetical Progression, whose first term is 2; the common difference 4, and number of terms 13?

number of terms 13—1 = 12   2 + 50 = 52 first & last terms.
  common difference 4   13 number of terms.

     ——   ——
     48   156
  first term. + 2   52

     ——   ——
  the last term. 50   2)676

  Sum of all the terms.   838 Answer.

2. A man sold 40 yards of linen, at 2 cents for the first yard, 4 cents for the second, increasing 2 cents every yard; what did they amount to?   Ans. $16 40cts.

3. Bought 15 yards of linen, at 2 cents for the first yard, 4 cents for the second, 6 cents for the third, &c., increasing 2 cents every yard; what was the cost of the last yard, and what was the cost of the whole?
    Ans. The last yd. cost 30cts,—the whole $2 40cts.

4. Twenty persons gave charity to a poor woman; the first gave 6 cents, the second 8 cents, and so on in arithmetical progression; how much did the last person give, and what sum did the woman receive?
    Ans. The last person gave 44 cts,—she received $5.

5. A man on a journey travels the first day 10 miles, the second 14 miles, increasing 4 miles every day; how many miles did he travel the tenth day, and how many miles did he travel in all?
    Ans. Tenth day 46 miles,—in all 280 miles.

6. Suppose a number of stones were laid a yard distant from each other for the space of a mile, and the first a yard from a basket; what length of ground will that man travel over who gathers them up singly, returning with them one by one to the basket?   **Ans. 1761 miles.**

CASE 2.

When the two extremes and the number of terms are given to find the common difference.

RULE.

Subtract the less extreme from the greater, and divide the remainder by one less than the number of terms; the quotient will be the common difference.

EXAMPLES.

7. The extremes being 20 and 40; and the number of terms 6; what is the common difference?

Number of terms 6   40 } Extremes.
          1   20 }

One less 5   5)20

          Ans. 4 Common.

8. A man had 10 sons whose several ages differed alike; the youngest was 3 years old, and the eldest 48; what was the common difference of their ages?   **Ans. 5 years.**

9. A man is to travel from Boston to a certain place in 9 days, and to go but 5 miles the first day, increasing every day by an equal excess, so that the last day's journey may be 37 miles. Required the daily increase.

          Ans. 4 miles.

10. A man received charity from 10 different persons; the first gave him 4 cents, the last 49 cents, in arithmetical progression; what was the common difference, and what did the man receive?

     Ans. Received $2 65cts.—common difference 5cts.

11. When a debt is paid at 8 different payments, in arithmetical progression, the first payment to be $21; the last $175; what is the common difference; and what each payment, and what was the whole debt?

Ans. Common difference, $22 — Second payment, $43 — Third payment, $65, &c.—The whole sum, $784.

GEOMETRICAL PROGRESSION.

Geometrical Progression is the increase of a series of numbers by a common multiplier, or decrease by a common divisor, as 4, 8, 16, 32, 64;—64, 32, 16, 8, 4. The multiplier or divisor by which any series is increased or decreased, is called the ratio.

CASE.

To find the last term and sum of the series.

RULE.

Raise the ratio to a power whose index is one less than the number of terms given in the sum. Multiply the product by the first term, and that product by the ratio. From this last product subtract the first term, and divide the remainder by a number that is one less than the ratio. The quotient will be the sum of the series.

EXAMPLES.

1. If I buy 18 bushels of wheat, and pay 2 cents for the first bushel, 4 for the second, 8 for the third, &c., doubling to the last, how much must I pay?

1st power.	2nd power.	3rd power.	4th power.	5th power.	6th power.	7th power.
Ratio 2,	4,	8;	16,	32,	64,	128,

```
                                          128
                                         ─────
                                         1024
                                          256
                                          128
                                         ─────
                            16384. 14th power.
                                8  3rd power.
                              ─────
                            131072  17th power.
                                 2  First term.
                            ──────
                            262144
                                 2  Ratio.
                            ──────
                            524288
                                 2  First term.
                            ──────
Divide by Ratio 2 — 1 = 1)524286

            Ans. $5242 86 cts.
```

2. A man taught school 21 days, and received for the first day 1 cent, for the second 2, for the third 4, and so on, until the last. What sum did he receive?
                    Ans. 20,971 dollars 51 cents.

3. A gentleman, whose daughter was married on a New Year's day, gave her $1, promising to triple it on the first day of each month in the year. What did her portion amount to?   Ans. $265,720.

4. What sum would purchase a horse with 4 shoes, and six nails in each shoe, at ¼ of a cent for the first nail, a half for the second, a cent for the third, &c., doubling to the last?   Ans. $41,943 03¾ cts.

5. A merchant sold 20 bushels of clover seed, at 1 cent for the first bushel, 4 for the second, 16 for the third, and

so on; in quadruple proportion. What sum did he receive, and how much did he gain by the sale, supposing he gave $5 per bushel for the seed?

Ans. $\begin{cases} \$3,665,038,759.25 \text{ cts. sum received.} \\ \$3,665,038,659.25 \text{ cts. gained.} \end{cases}$

COMPOUND INTEREST, BY DECIMALS.

The ratio in Compound Interest is the amount of 1 dollar for 1 year, which is found as follows:

100 : 104 : : 1   (104 amount for 1 year at 4 per cent.

Note. The 4th root of the ratio will be the quarterly amount—the square root the half yearly amount—and the product arising from the half yearly and quarter yearly, multiplied together, the three quarter yearly amount, as follows:

Thus: $\sqrt[4]{1.04} = 1.009853$, quarterly amount; and $\sqrt[2]{1.04} = 1.019804$, half yearly amount; then $1.009853 \times 1.019804 = 1.029852$, amount for 3qrs. of a year, at 4 per cent.

Note. The 4th root is found by extracting the square root of the square root. The ratio involved to the power, whose index is the time, is the amount of one dollar for that time, as a square for two years, a cube for three years, &c.

Thus: $1.04 \times 1.04 \times 1.04 = 1.124864$, amount of 1 dollar for three years, at 4 per cent.

When the ratio is to be involved to years and quarters, the power for the years must be multiplied by the quarterly amount.

Thus: $1.1910160 \times 1.014674 = 1.2184929$, amount for 3¼ years, at 6 per cent.

The power of 1 dollar may also be obtained for months and days, nearly, by adding the monthly simple interest of

1 dollar, or proper parts thereof, to the amount of the quarter next preceding the given time, for what that time exceeds the said quarter, as follows:

Amount for ½ year, =1.029563: For 4¼ years, =1.318873
Int. of $1 for 1mo., = .005000 ——————— .005000
One sixth for 5 days, = .000833 ——————— .000833

For 7 months, 5 days=1.035396.for4y.10mo.5d.=1.824706

TABLE I.

Amount of $1 for a year, and for Quarters, at Compound Interest.

Rate pr. ct.	Ratio.	For three Quarters.	For two Quarters.	For one Quarter.	Simple Int. of $1 for 1 month.
3	1.03	1.022416	1.014889	1.007417	.002500
3½	1.035	1.026137	1.017349	1.008637	.002917
4	1.04	1.029852	1.019804	1.009858	.003333
4½	1.045	1.033563	1.022252	1.011065	.003750
5	1.05	1.037270	1.024695	1.012272	.004167
5½	1.055	1.040973	1.027132	1.013475	.004583
6	1,06	1.044671	1.029536	1.014674	.005000
6½	1.065	1.048364	1.031988	1.015868	.005417
7	1.07	1.052053	1.034408	1.017058	.005833

TABLE 2. Showing the amount of one dollar from one year to forty.

yr.	6 per cent.	4½ per cent.	5 per cent.	5½ per cent.	6 per cent.
1	1.0400000	1.0450000	1.0500000	1.0550000	1.0600000
2	1.0816000	1.0920250	1.1025000	1.1130250	1.1360000
3	1.1248640	1.1411661	1.1576250	1.1742413	1.1910160
4	1.1698585	1.1925186	1.2155062	1.2388246	1.2624769
5	1.2166529	1.2461819	1.2762815	1.3069598	1.3382256
6	1.2653190	1.3022601	1.3400956	1.3788426	1.4185191
7	1.3159317	1.3608618	1.4071004	1.4546789	1.5036302
8	1.3685690	1.4221006	1.4774554	1.5346862	1.5938480
9	1.4233118	1.4860951	1.5513282	1.6190939	1.6894789
10	1.4802442	1.5529694	1.6288946	1.7081440	1.7908476
11	1.5394540	1.6228530	1.7103393	1.8020919	1.8982985
12	1.6010322	1.6958814	1.7958563	1.9012069	2.0121964
13	1.6650735	1.7721961	1.8856491	2.0057732	2.1329282
14	1.7316764	1.8519449	1.9799316	2.1160907	2.2609039
15	1.8009435	1.9352824	2.0789281	2.2324756	2.3965581
16	1.8729812	2.0223701	2.1828745	2.3552617	2.5403517
17	1.9479005	2.1133768	2.2930183	2.4848011	2.6927727
18	2.0258161	2.2084787	2.4066192	2.6214652	2.8543391
19	2.1068491	2.3078603	2.5269502	2.7656458	3.0255995
20	2.1911231	2.4117140	2.6532977	2.9177563	3.2071355
21	2.2787680	2.5202411	2.7859625	3.0782329	3.3995636
22	2.3699187	2.6336520	2.9252607	3.2475357	3.6035374
23	2.4647155	2.7521663	3.0715237	3.4261502	3.8097496
24	2.5633041	2.8760138	3.2250999	3.6145885	4.0489346
25	2.6658363	3.0054344	3.3863549	3.8133919	4.2918707
26	2.7724697	3.1406790	3.5556726	4.0231279	4.5493829
27	2.8833685	3.2820095	3.7334563	4.2443999	4.8223459
28	2.9987033	3.4296999	3.9201291	4.4778419	5.1116867
29	3.1186514	3.5840364	4.1161356	4.7241232	5.4183870
30	3.2433975	3.7453181	4.3219428	4.9839469	5.7434912
31	3.3734324	3.9138574	4.5380394	5.2580671	6.0881007
32	3.5080587	4.0899810	4.7649414	5.5472608	6.4533867
33	3.6481831	4.2740301	5.0031885	5.8523600	6.8405899
34	3.7943168	4.4663015	5.2533473	6.1742398	7.2510253
35	3.9460889	4.6673478	5.5160152	6.5138230	7.6860868
36	4.1030325	4.8773784	5.7918101	6.8720832	8.1472520
37	4.2680898	5.0968604	6.0314069	7.2500478	8.6360871
38	4.4388134	5.3262192	6.3854772	7.6488004	9.1542523
39	4.6163659	5.5658990	6.7047511	8.0694844	9.7035074
40	4.8010206	5.8163645	7.0399887	8.5133060	10.2857178

Compound Interest is that in which the interest of 1 year is added to the principal, and that amount is the principal for the second year, and so on for any number of years.

CASE I.

The principal, time and rate given to find the amount.

RULE.

Multiply the principal by the ratio involved to the time, which may be taken from table 2, and the product will be the amount, from which subtract the principal for the compound interest.

EXAMPLES.

1. What is the compound interest and amount of $300 for 3 years, at 5 per cent.?

$$1.05 \times 1.05 \times 1.05 = 1.1576250$$
$$300$$

$$\text{Answer.} \begin{cases} \$347.28.7.5000 \text{ amount.} \\ 300 \\ \overline{\$47.28.7 \text{ interest.}} \end{cases}$$

2. What is the amount of $500 for five years, at 6 per cent.?   Ans. $669.11.2.

3. What is the compound interest of $100 for four years, at 5 per cent.?   Ans. $21.55.

4. What is the amount of five dollars for 20 years, at six per cent.?   Ans. $16.03.5.

5. What is the compound interest of 1000 dollars for thirteen years, at six per cent. per annum?   Ans. $1132.92.8.

6. What is the amount of 50 dollars for 11 years, at 6 per cent.?   Ans. $94.91.4m. +

7. What is the amount of 12 dollars for one half year, at 6 per cent.?   Ans. $12.35.4.

CASE 2.

The amount, time, and rate per cent. given to find the principal.

RULE.

Divide the amount by the ratio involved to the time in table 2.

EXAMPLES.

1. What principal, put to interest, will amount to $400 in five years, at 6 per cent. ?

- 1.3382256)400:0000000   Ans. $298.90.3.

2. What principal, put to interest, will amount to $1500 in 7 years, at 5½ per cent. ?   Ans. $1031.15½. +

PERMUTATION

Permutation is used to show how many ways things may be varied in place or succession.

RULE.

Multiply all the terms of the series continually, from one to the given number, inclusive, and the last product will be the answer required.

EXAMPLES.

1. In how many different positions can ten persons place themselves round a table ?

$1 \times 2 \times 3 \times 4 \times 5 \times 6 \times 7 \times 8 \times 9 \times 10 = $ **Ans.** 3628800.

2. The church in Boston has 8 bells; how many changes may be rung on them ?   Ans. 40320.

3. In what time will a person make all the changes that the first 12 letters of the alphabet admit of, allowing 15 seconds to each change, and 365¼ days to a year.
Ans. 227y. 248da. 6h.

COMBINATION

Combination is used to show how many different ways a less number of things can be combined out of a greater, as out of the figures 1, 2, 3, 4; four combinations, 12, 21, 34 and 43, may be performed.

RULE.

Take a series proceeding from and increasing by a unit up to the number to be combined. Take another series of as many places decreasing by unity from the number out of which the combinations are to be made. Multiply the first continually for a divisor, and the last for a dividend, the quotient will be the answer.

EXAMPLES.

1. How many combinations of 4 persons in 8 ?

$$1 \times 2 \times 3 \times 4 = 24 \qquad 24)1680(70 \text{ Ans.}$$
$$8 \times 7 \times 6 \times 5 = 1680 \qquad 168$$
$$\overline{0}$$

2. How many combinations of 10 figures may be made out of 20?   Ans. 184756.

3. How many changes may be rung with 10 bells out of 20?   Ans. 184756.

DUODECIMALS.

Duodecimals are parts of a foot; the denominations of which increase continually by 12. The denominations are,

12 fourths ('''') make	1 third.'''
12 thirds	1 second.''
12 seconds	1 inch. in.
12 inches	1 foot. ft

ADDITION OF DUODECIMALS.

RULE.

Proceed as in Compound Addition, observing to carry one for every 12.

EXAMPLES.

		ft.	in.	''	'''			ft.	in.	''	'''	''''
(1.)		6	4	2	1	(2.)		40	7	1	9	6
		8	10	9	11			22	8	7	1	4
		13	7	10	8			15	11	9	8	10
		19	15	5	2			1	3	0	0	1
Ans.		49	2	3	5	Ans.		80	6	6	7	9

3. Three planks measure as follows: 16ft. 8in. — 14ft. 6in.—17ft. 9in. 2'' How many feet do they contain?

Ans. 48ft. 11in. 2''.

SUBTRACTION OF DUODECIMALS.

RULE.

Proceed as in Compound Subtraction, observing the 12's.

EXAMPLES.

	ft.	in.	''	'''	''''			ft.	in.	''	'''	''''
(1.)	50	2	11	9	1	(2.)		400	8	7	11	0
	17	5	10	11	4			387	9	6	1	4
Ans.	32	9	0	9	9	Ans.		12	11	1	9	8

3. If 19ft. 10in. be cut off from a board which contains 41ft. 7in., how much will be left?　　Ans. 21ft. 9in.

MULTIPLICATION OF DUODECIMALS.

RULE.

Set the multiplier in such a manner that the feet thereof may stand under the lowest denomination of the multiplicand; multiply and carry one for every 12 from one denomination to another; and take parts for the inches, as in Practice.

Note. Feet multiplied by feet, give feet.
　　　Feet multiplied by inches, give inches.
　　　Feet multiplied by seconds, give seconds.
　　　Inches multiplied by inches, give seconds.
　　　Inches multiplied by seconds, give thirds.
　　　Seconds multiplied by seconds, give fourths.

EXAMPLES.

1. Multiply 5ft. 6in. by 2ft. 4in.

$$
\begin{array}{ccc}
in. & ft. & in. \\
4 \mid \frac{1}{3} \mid & 5 & 6 \\
& & 2 \\
\hline
& 11 & 0 \\
& 1 & 10 \\
\end{array}
$$

Ans.   12ft. 10in.

2. Multiply 54ft. 10in. by 5ft. 7in.   Ans. 306ft. 1in. 10′
3. Multiply 9ft. 7in. by 3ft. 6in.   Ans. 33ft. 6in. 6″.
4. What are the contents of a door, measuring in length 6ft. 9in. 3″, and in width 3ft. 5in.?

Ans. 23ft. 1in. 7″ 3‴.

5. A certain partition is 81ft. 10in. 4″ long, and 14ft. 7in. 5″ high. How many yards does it contain?

Ans. 132yd. 8ft. 7in. 9″ 7‴ 8‴″.

6. If a floor be 79ft. 4in. by 38ft. 11in., how many square feet are there in it?   Ans. 3100ft. 4in. 4″
7. How many square feet in a board 17ft. 7in. long, and 1ft. 5in. wide?   Ans. 24ft. 10in. 11″
8. What will be the expense of plastering the walls of a room 8ft. 6in. high, and each of the four sides 16ft. 3in. long, at 50 cents per square yard?   Ans. $30 69. +
9. In 40 planks, 13ft. long and 8in. wide, how many feet?   Ans. 346⅔ft.
10. In 49 planks, 22ft. long and 11in. wide, how many feet?   Ans. 988ft. 2in.
11. In 17 planks, 12ft. long and 5in. wide, how many feet?   Ans. 85 feet.

PROMISCUOUS EXAMPLES.

1. How many bushels of corn, at 22 cents per bushel, can I have for 40 dollars?   Ans. 181 2/11 bu.
2. If a man's yearly income be $7777, how much is it per day?   Ans. $21 30cts. 6m. +
3. My agent sends me word he has bought goods to the

value of 500 dollars 54cts. upon my account; what will his commission come to at 4 per cent.?

Ans. 20 dollars 2cts. +

4. A man had in his desk 2176 dollars 55 cents, he drew out at one time 13 dollars 6¼ cents, at another time 49 dollars 1 cent, and at another 61 dollars 21¾ cts., after which he deposited at one time 88 dollars 88¼ cts.; how much had he in desk after making the deposit?

Ans. $2142 14¼ cents.

5. A. is 25 years old, B. 15 years older than A., and C. is 12 years older than B. The ages of B. and C. are required?

Ans. B. 40y. C. 52y.

6. Sold 6 bales of cloth, 5 of which contained 10 pieces each, and in each piece were 28 yards; the other bale contained 16 pieces, and in each piece were 20 yards. How many pieces and how many yards were there in all?

Ans. 66 pieces, and 1720 yds.

7. If goods which cost 44 dollars, be sold for 62 dollars, what is the gain per cent.? Ans. 40$\frac{9}{11}$ per cent.

8. If $\frac{4}{7}$ of an ounce cost $\frac{7}{8}$ of a dollar, what will $\frac{4}{5}$ of a pound cost? Ans. $19 60 cts.

9. If $\frac{3}{8}$ of a gallon cost 1$\frac{1}{9}$ dollars, what will $\frac{8}{11}$ of a ton come to? Ans. $610 90 cts. 9m. +

10. A person who was possessed of $\frac{4}{5}$ of a store, sold $\frac{4}{9}$ of his share for 551 dollars 62½ cents, what was the whole store worth at that rate? Ans. 1241 dollars 15½ cents.

11. What will 27cwt. of iron come to at $4 56 cts. per cwt.? Ans. $123 12 cts.

12. If I buy 100 yards of cloth, at 50 cents per yard, at how much must I sell it per yard to gain 100 per cent.?

Ans. $1.

13. Bought a quantity of goods for $400, and 5 months afterwards sold them for $650. How much per cent. per annum was gained by the transaction?

Ans. 150 per cent.

14. What is the interest of $51 62½ cents for 2 years, 3 months, and 13 days, at 7½ per cent.?

Ans. $8 85 cents. +

15. How often would a wagon-wheel turn round in rolling from Knoxville to Baltimore; suppose the distance to be 600 miles; admitting the wheel be 5 feet in diameter?

Ans. 201600 times.

16. A person has two silver cups of unequal weight, having one cover for both which weighs 5oz., now if the cover be put on the less cup it will be double the weight of the greater cup, and put on the greater cup it will be three times as heavy as the less cup, what is the weight of each cup? Ans. The less 3 oz., the greater 4 oz.

17. A man had $20, which he wished to lay out as follows: viz., in sugar at 10 cents, coffee at 14 cents, and rice at 11 cents per pound; so as to have an equal quantity of each. How many pounds must he have? Ans. 57¼ lb.

18. A corn-crib is 5ft. wide at the bottom, and 7ft. wide at the top, tell me how wide it is on an average?
Ans. 6 feet.

19. When $25 are multiplied by $25, how much money is there in the product? Ans. $625.

20. When $25 are multiplied by 25 cents, how much money is there in the product? Ans. $6 25 cts.

21. When 25 cents are multiplied by 25 cents, how much money is there in the product? Ans. 6¼ cents.

22. How much will 18¾ bushels of corn come to at 18¾ cents per bushel? Ans. $3 51 cts. 5m.+

23. What will 2½ pounds of beef come to at 2½ cents per pound? Ans. 6¼ cents.

24. In 48 planks 8 inches wide and 10 feet long, how many feet? Ans. 320 feet.

25. A house is 20 feet long, and 18 feet wide. How many feet of plank will be required to cover the floor?
Ans. 360 feet.

26. What is the neat of a hog weighing 294 pounds gross? Ans. 256½ lb. neat.

27. If A. can drink a pint of whiskey in 20 minutes; B. one in 30; and C. one in 40; in what time can they drink a pint, when all drinking together?

Divide by 20, 30, and 40. Suppose 120

$$\frac{3}{4}$$
$$6$$

13)120(Ans. $9\frac{3}{13}$ min.
117

Note. In any question like the above, suppose any number into which all the given numbers may be divided without any remainder, then add together their quotients, by which sum divide the same dividend. The quotient will be the answer.

28. Three young ladies met at their neighbours' for the purpose of finishing a fine quilt. Said M., I can finish it in six hours; said E., I can do it in four hours; said L., I can do it in three hours; but we will all work together. In what time can we finish the quilt? Ans. $1\frac{1}{3}$ hours.

29. There is a cellar dug, that is 20 feet every way in length, breadth and depth. How many solid feet of earth were taken out of it? Ans. 8000 feet.

30. How many bricks, 9 inches long and 4 inches wide, will pave a yard that is 300 feet long and 40 feet wide? Ans. 48000 bricks.

31. What sum will produce as much interest in five years, as $500 would in 8 years and 4 months? Ans. $$833\frac{1}{3}$.

32. A guardian paid his ward $3500 for $2500, which he had held in possession 8 years. What rate of interest did he allow him? Ans. 5.

33. A. owes B. 100 dollars, payable in $3\frac{1}{4}$ months; $150 in $4\frac{1}{2}$ months, and $204 in $5\frac{3}{4}$ months; but is willing to make one payment of the whole. In what time should the payment be made? Ans. 4mo. 23 days. +

34. In what time will any sum of money double itself, at 5 per cent., simple interest? Ans. 20 years.

35. If B. can do a piece a work alone in 10 days, and C. can do it in 19 days, in what time can they finish it, both working together? Ans. $6\frac{16}{29}$ days.

36. A. B. and C. found a purse of money, containing $60; whereof A. is to have $\frac{1}{2}$, B. $\frac{1}{3}$, and C. $\frac{1}{4}$. What will be the share of each?

Ans. { A.'s share $27 69 cents 2m. +
B.'s share $18 46 cents 1m. +
C.'s share $13 84 cents 6m. + }

37. A. and B. traded together; A. put in 320 dollars for five months; B. put in 460 dollars for 3 months; and they

gained 100 dollars. What was each man's share of the gain?

Ans. $\begin{cases} \text{A.'s share \$53 69cts. 1m. +} \\ \text{B.'s share \$46 30cts. 8m. +} \end{cases}$

30. What is the difference between the interest of $1000, at 6 per cent. for 8 years, and the discount of the same sum for the same time, and at the same rate of interest?

Ans. The int. exceeds the discount by $155 67cts. 5m.

39. Said Dick to Harry, I can place four nines in such a manner that they will make precisely an even hundred. Can you do so too? Ans. 99$\frac{9}{9}$.

40. What is the sum of third and half the third of 6$\frac{1}{4}$ cents? Ans. 3$\frac{1}{8}$ cents.

41. How many dollars are there in £200, Tennessee currency? Ans. $666 61$\frac{2}{3}$ cents.

42. The clocks of Italy go on to 24 hours. How many strokes do they strike in one complete revolution of the index? Ans. 300.

43. A line 40 yards long will exactly reach from the top of a fort, standing on the brink of a river, to the opposite bank, known to be 25 yards from the foot of the wall. What is the height of the wall? Ans. 31.22yds.

44. What is the value of a slab of marble, the length of which is 5ft. 7in. and the breadth 1ft. 10in., at $2 per foot? Ans. $20 47cts. +

45. Shipped to New Orleans 4000lb. of cotton, at 7$\frac{1}{2}$ cts. per lb., and 513 yards of muslin, at 62$\frac{1}{2}$ cts per yard; in return for which, I have received 37cwt. 3qr. of sugar, at 12$\frac{1}{2}$ cents per pound, and 44 pounds of indigo, at 20 cents per pound. What remains due to me?

Ans. $83 33$\frac{1}{2}$ cents.

46. If the flash of a gun was observed just 1 minute and 20 seconds before the report: What was the distance, supposing the flash to be seen the instant of its going off, and admitting the sound to fly at the rate of 1150 feet in a second? Ans. 17m. 3fur. 15p. 4yd. 0ft. 6in.

47. There is a certain pole, $\frac{1}{2}$ of which is in the water, $\frac{1}{3}$ in the mud, and 6ft. on dry ground. What is the whole length of the pole? Ans. 36ft.

48. When $\frac{1}{2}$ of the number of an Assembly, and 15, were met, there were $\frac{1}{3}$ and 10 absent. How many did that branch of the legislature consist of? Ans. 150.

49. Bought goods for $500, and sold the same immediately for $400. What was the loss per cent.?

Ans. 20 per cent.

50. What is the interest of $15,000,000 for one minute, at 6 per cent. per annum? Ans. $1 71 cts. 2m. +

51. If the earth be 360 degrees in circumference, and each degree 60 miles, how long would a man be in travelling round it, who advances 40 miles a day, reckoning 365¼ days a year? Ans. 1y. 174da. 18hr.

52. Sold 12 yards of cloth for $15 20cts., by which was gained 8 per cent. What was the first cost of a yard?

Ans. $1 17cts. 2m. +

53. Bought 12 pieces of white cloth for $16 50cts. per piece; paid $2 87cts. per piece for dying. For how much must I sell them each, to gain 20 per cent.?

Ans. $23 24cts. 4m.

54. When I, by disposing of a yard of cloth at $7, gain 56¼ cents, what would I gain by selling 3 pieces, which cost me $400? Ans. 32 14¼cts. +

55. The yearly interest of Charlotte's money at 6 per cent. per annum exceeds one twentieth part of the principal by $100, and she does not intend to marry any man who is not scholar enough to tell her fortune. Pray what is it?

Ans. $10,000.

56. There is a cistern having eight pipes to discharge it. By the first it may be emptied in ten minutes; by the second in 20; by the third in 40; by the 4th in 80; by the 5th in 160; by the 6th in 320; by the 7th in 640; and by the 8th in 1280. In what time will all eight running together empty it? Ans. 5$\frac{1}{15}$ minutes.

57. In 140 planks, each 12 feet long and 9 inches wide, how many feet? Ans. 1260.

58. At a certain quilting, ½ of the girls are eating, ⅓ of them cooking, and 5 at work; I would know how many girls there are at the place? Ans. 30.

59. A hare starts 12 rods before a hound, but is not perceived by him till she has been up 45 seconds. She scuds away at the rate of 10 miles an hour, and the dog on view, makes after at the rate of 16 miles an hour. How long will the course hold, and what space will be run over from the spot whence the dog started, until the hare be overtaken? Ans. 2288ft. and 97½ sec.

60. Bought a watch at 10 per cent. under its value, and sold it at 10 per cent. over its value, and by so doing gained $10. How much was the watch worth? Ans. $50.

61. Bought a horse and saddle for $100. The horse was worth seven times as much as the saddle. How much was the horse worth, and how much was the saddle worth?

Ans. $\begin{cases} \text{H. } \$87\ 50. \\ \text{S. } \$12\ 50. \end{cases}$

62. A. owes B. 100 bushels of corn, the tub out of which they expect to measure the same, contains 1bu. 1pe. 1qt. 1pt. How often must it be filled to make the 100 bushels?

Ans. $77\frac{9}{83}$.

63. A merchant purchased 200 yards of broad cloth, at $3 per yard. A customer who was desirous of speculating, proposed to take $300 worth of the cloth, at $2 75 per yard, and then give $3 25 for the remainder. What would the merchant gain or lose by the transaction?

Ans. He would lose $4 54.$\frac{6}{11}$.

APPENDIX.

MENSURATION OF SURFACES.

To find the area of a Parallelogram, Square, Rhombus or Rhomboid.

Multiply the length by the perpendicular height or breadth.

EXAMPLES.

1. How many square feet are there in a floor $23\frac{1}{2}$ feet long and 18 feet broad?   Ans. $23\frac{1}{2} \times 18 = 423$.

2. What are the contents of a piece of ground 66 poles square?   Ans. 4356po. or 27a. 36po.

3. What are the contents of a rhombus, whose sides are 60 feet, and perpendicular 50 feet?

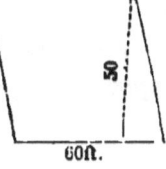

Ans. 3000 feet.

4. How many acres are there in a field in the form of a rhomboid, the sides of which are 50 poles, and perpendicular distance 25 poles?   Ans. 7a. 3r. 10p.

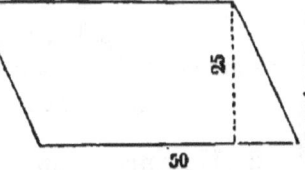

5. How many square feet are there in a plank 13 feet long and 7in. broad?   Ans. 7ft. 84in.

6. How many square feet are there in a plank 18 feet long, 12 inches at one end and 8 inches at the other?   Ans. 15 feet.

$$12 + 8 = 20 \div 2 = 10$$

```
         6 | ½ | 18 feet.
         4 | 4 |  9
               |  6
               ------
            15 Ans.
```

7 How many square feet are there in 20 planks, 15 feet long, and each 9 inches wide?   Ans. 225 feet.

Note. When there is a number of planks to be calculated of the same length and breadth, multiply the width of one in inches by the number of planks, divide the product by 12, and multiply by the length.

$$9 \times 20 = 180 \div 12 = 15 \times 1\tfrac{1}{2} = 225.$$

8. How many square feet are there in 50 pieces of scantling, 4 inches by 3, counting one side and edge, and 20 feet long?   Ans. 583⅓ feet.

$$4 + 3 = 7 \times 50 = 350 \div 12 = 29\tfrac{1}{6} \times 20 = 583\tfrac{1}{3} \text{ feet.}$$

9. How many square feet are there in 30 pieces of scantling 14 feet long, 4 inches by 2?   Ans. 210 feet.

To find the area of a Triangle.

Multiply one side by half the perpendicular from the opposite angle.

EXAMPLES.

1. If A. B. be 65 poles, and the perpendicular 31 poles, how many acres are contained in the Triangle?

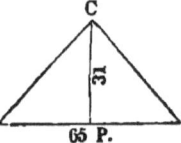

$$31 \div 2 = 15\tfrac{1}{2} \times 65 = 1007\tfrac{1}{2}\text{po. or 6a. 1r. 7}\tfrac{1}{2}\text{p.}$$

2. How many square feet are there in a triangle whose base is 120 feet and perpendicular 75 feet?   Ans. 4500.

To find the circumference of a circle from its diameter.

Multiply the diameter by 3.14159, or multiply the diameter by 355, and divide the product by 113.

EXAMPLES.

1. If the diameter of the earth be 7930 miles, what is the circumference?   Ans. 7930 × 3.14159 = 24912.8 miles.

2. How many miles does the earth move, in revolving round the sun; supposing the orbit to be a circle whose diameter is 190 millions of miles?   Ans. 596.902.604

To find the diameter of a circle from its circumference.

Divide the circumference by 3.14159; or multiply the circumference 113, and divide the product by 355.

EXAMPLES.

1. What is the diameter of a tree which is 5½ feet round?
$$3.14159)5.5000000(1.75 \text{ Ans.}$$
2. If the circumference of the sun be 2.800.000 miles, what is its diameter?   Ans. 891.267

To find the area of a Circle.

Multiply the square of the diameter by the decimals .7854.

EXAMPLES.

1. What is the surface of a circular fish-pond which is 10 poles in diameter? $10 \times 10 \times .7854 = 78.54$ Ans.
2. What is the area of a circle whose diameter is 623 feet?   Ans. 304836.
3. How many acres are there in a circular island whose diameter is 124 poles?   Ans. 75a. 76po.

To find the area of an elipsis or oval.

Multiply the longest diameter by the shortest, and that product by 7854.

EXAMPLES.

1. What is the area of an oval whose greatest diameter is 36 feet, and least 28?
$$28 \times 36 \times .7854 = 791.68 \text{ feet Ans}$$

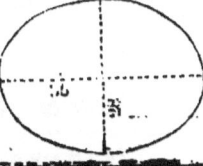

MENSURATION OF SOLIDS

In solid measure 1728　　cubic inches$=1$ cubic foot.
　　　　　　　　282　　cubic inches$=1$ ale gallon.,
　　　　　　　　231　　cubic inches$=1$ wine gallon.
　　　　　　150.42 cubic inches$=1$ bushel.

1 cubic foot of pure water weighs $62\frac{1}{2}$ pounds.

To find the solidity of a piece of hewn timber, box, &c

Multiply the length, breadth, and depth or height, together.

EXAMPLES.

1. How many solid feet are there in a piece of square timber 3 feet by 2, and 20 feet long?
$$3 \times 2 \times 20 = 120 \text{ feet Ans.}$$
2. How many cubic inches are there in a piece of marble in a cubic form, which is 12 inches every way?
$$12 \times 12 \times 12 = 1728 \text{ Ans.}$$
3. How many cubic quarters of an inch are there in one cubic inch?　　　　　　　　　　　　　　　Ans. 64.
4. What is the solidity of a wall 22 feet long, 12 feet high, and 2 feet 6 inches thick?　　　　　　Ans. 660.
5. How many cubic inches are there in a box 2 feet at the bottom,* 3 feet at the top, 4 feet high, and 6 feet long?
　　　　　　　　　　　　　　　　　　Ans. 103680.

To find the number of bushels or gallons contained in a corn-house or box, ascertain how many cubic inches are contained in the box or house, and divide them by the number of inches in a bushel or gallon. If the house contain ears of corn, divide the number of bushels by 2, which will give the number of shelled corn.

EXAMPLES.

1. How many ale gallons are there in a cistern, which is

In all such examples take the average width or length.

11 feet 9 inches deep, and whose base is 4 feet 2 inches square?

Ans. $\begin{cases} \text{The cistern contains 352500 cubic inches.} \\ \text{And } 352500 \div 2.2 = 1250 \text{ gallons.} \end{cases}$

2. How many wine gallons will fill a ditch 3 feet 11 inches wide, 3 feet deep, and 462 feet long?   Ans 40608.

3. How many bushels of corn are there in a crib 5 feet wide, 5 feet high and 10 feet long, filled with ears?

Ans. 100bu. 1½p. +

4. How many bushels of corn are there in a crib 20 feet long, 10 feet deep, and 6 feet wide?   Ans. 481¼. +

Note. As complete accuracy is not to be expected from any rule to gauge a crib, the following is recommended as being accurate enough for practice.   Multiply the number of cubic feet in a crib by 2, and divide the product by 5. Take the above example,

$$2 \times 10 \times 6 = 1200 \times 2 = 2400 \div 5 = 480.$$

5. How many bushels of corn are there in a crib 15 feet long, 10 feet high, 8 feet wide at the bottom, and 6 at the top?   Ans. 480.

6. How many bushels of coal will a coal bed contain, 14 feet long, 4 feet wide, and 3 feet 6 inches high?

Ans. 156⅘.

Note. In such examples, it will produce very near the true result to multiply the number of cubic feet by 4, and divide the product by 5.

————

To make a box large enough to contain a given quantity, multiply the number of bushels or gallons to be contained by the number of cubic inches in a bushel or gallon.   If the box is to be in a cubic form, extract the cube root of the product.   If the side or end of the box be given to ascertain how long or wide it must be, divide the product by the number of square inches contained by the side or end.

EXAMPLES.

1. It is required to make a box in a cubic form large

enough to contain 1 bushel. How many inches must it be every way?

The cube root of $2150 = 12.9 +$ in. make it 13 in. every way.

2. How large a box in the form of a cube will contain ½ bushel?   Ans. $10.29 +$ or $10\frac{1}{4}$ in. nearly.

3. How large a box, in a cubic form, will contain 5 bushels?   Ans. $22 +$ in.

4. How long must a box be made to contain 50 bushels, which is to be 4 feet wide and 3 feet high?

                         Ans. 5 feet 2.2 in.

$2150 \times 50 = 107500 \div 1728 = 62.2 = 5\text{ft}.2.2\text{in}.36 \times 48 = 1728$

5. What must be the length of a box, the end of which is 3 feet by 2, to contain 20 bushels?   Ans. 5 feet 1½ in.

6. How wide must a box be made, which is to be 10 feet long and 5 feet deep?   Ans. 4 feet 11.72 in.

To find the solidity of a Cylinder.

Multiply the area of one end by the length.

EXAMPLES.

1. What is the solidity of a cylinder whose length is 60 inches and diameter 20 inches?

     $20 \times 20 = 400 \times .7854 = 3141600 \times 60 = 18849.6$ Ans.

2. What is the solidity of a cylinder whose length is 121 inches and diameter 45.2 inches?   Ans. 194156.6.

3. The Winchester bushel is a hollow cylinder 18½ inches in diameter and 8 inches deep?   Ans. 2150.42.

4. How many cubic feet are there in a log of timber 2 feet in diameter and 20 feet long?   Ans. 62.83.

5. A gentleman has a bushel measure which is 15 inches in diameter and 12 inches deep, how much is it too great or too small?   Ans. { 29.84 inches, or a little more than a pint, wine measure.

6. A gentleman has purchased a gallon measure in the form of a cylinder, which is 6 inches in diameter and 10 inches deep. He was told it was a wine measure by the merchant. Is it a correct measure?

         Ans. { It contains 282.7 cubic inches therefore it must be ale measure.

To find the contents of a vessel in the shape of a frustrum of a cone.

Square the diameter of each end, multiply their squares together, and extract the square root of their product, to which add the two squares, and then multiply by the decimals .7854 and ⅓ of the length.

EXAMPLES.

1. How many cubic inches are contained in a vessel 9 inches deep, 4 inches in diameter at the bottom, and 3 feet at the top?   Ans. 87.18 cubic inches.

$4 \times 4 = 16$ $3 \times 3 = 9 \times 16 = 144$ the square root is 12
$9 + 16 + 12 = 37 \times .7854 = 29.0598 \times 3 = 87.18$ cubic in.

2. A measure which has been made for a wine gallon is 6 inches at the bottom, 5 inches at the top, and 10 deep. Is it a correct measure?

Ans. { It contains 238 cubic inches, 7 cubic inches too much, or 1 gill nearly.

3. A measure which has been made to contain ½ bushel is 12 inches at the bottom, 15 inches at the top, and 15 inches high.   Is it a correct measure?
Ans. It contains 1019.7 cubic inches, 56 too little.

4. How many gallons, wine measure, will a large crout tub contain, 9 feet high, 4 feet at the bottom, and 3 at the top?   Ans. 87.18 cubic feet, or 652.15 wine gallons.

GAUGING OF CASKS.

There are commonly reckoned four varieties of casks, for each of which some have a different rule, but the following rule will apply to all:

To calculate the contents of a cask, reduce the dimensions to inches; subtract the head from the bung diameter, multiply the difference by the decimal .7, if there be much curve of the staves betwixt the head and bung, by .67, if a little more than common, .6, if common, .57, if but little, .52, if none.   To this product add the head diameter.   Square their sum, which multip y by the decimals .0028, when ale, and .0034, when wine g allons are required, and the length of the cask.

Note. .0028 and .0084 are the results of dividing .7854 by 282 and 231.

EXAMPLES.

1. What is the capacity of a cask which has much curve betwixt the head and l ung, 30 inches long, head diameter 18, and bung 24 inches.'

Ans. 50.26 wine, or 41.3 ale gallons.

$$24-18=6\times 7=4.2+!8=22.2\times 22.2=4928.34\times .0034$$
$$=16.75656\times 30=50.2 \text{39680 gallons.}$$

2. How many wine gallons will a cask contain, of common curvature, which i. 30 inches long, head diameter 18, and bung 24 inches?   Ans. 45.9 gallons.

3. What is the capacity of a cask without curvature betwixt the head and bung, 30 inches in length, head diameter 18, and bung 24 inches'

Ans. 37.3 ale, or 45.3 wine gallons.

4. How many wine gallons will a cask contain, of the common form, whose ler gth is 27 inches, head diameter 21, and bung 23 inches?   Ans. 46.24 gallons.

TONNAGE OF FLAT BOATS.

The quantity which any vessel will carry is equal in weight to the quantity of water which the vessel displaces by loading; therefore the number of cubic feet of water displaced by loading a vessel, multiplied by 62½, will give the number of pounds which that vessel will carry.

To ascertain how many tons, barrels, &c., of a certain weight, a Flat Boat will carry

RULE.

Subtract ⅓ the rake or rakes from the length. Multiply the remainder by the depth to which she is sunk by the load, and that product by the width measured from the outside of the gunnels. If the product is not in feet, reduce it to feet, which multiply by 32½, which will give the number of pounds, which reduce to tons, or divide by the weight of a barrel, &c.

EXAMPLES.

1. How much will a flat boat carry which is 50 feet long, rake 10 feet, 12 feet wide, and will bear sinking 1½ feet?

Ans. 22 tons 12 cwt.

$50 - 5 = 45 \times 1\frac{1}{2} = 67\frac{1}{2} \times 12 = 810 \times 62\frac{1}{2} = 50625 \div 112 = 452 \div 20 = 22$ ton. 12 cwt.

2. What number of flour barrels, which weigh 196 pounds each, will a flat boat carry which is capable of being sunk 1 foot 3 inches, 50 feet long, one rake 10 feet, the other 8 feet, 15 feet wide? Ans. 515.

TABLES.

Of the present state of real and imaginary monies of the most commercial parts of the world, with the *United States*, and reduced to the value of the monies thereof, in Dollars, Cents and Mills.

This mark † is prefixed to the imaginary money, or money of account.

This mark = is *make*, or *equal* to.

In the column of Mills, wherever a figure is preceded by a point (.) it converts it to decimals: Thus 6.8 means *six* mills and *eight-tenths* of a mill.

		Dolls.	Cents.	Mills.
AMERICA				
UNITED STATES.				
A †Mill .				1
5 Mills = a half cent ...				5
10 Mills a cent ...			1	
5 Cents a half dime ..			5	
2 Half dimes a dime .			10	
25 Cents a ¼ of a dollar . .			25	
50 Cents a half dollar . ..			50	
10 Dimes a dollar		1		
2½ Dollars a ¼ eagle		2	50	
5 Dollars a ½ eagle . .		5		
10 Dollars an eagle		10		

Accounts, in the United States, are kept in Dollars and Cents.

CANADA, NOVA SCOTIA, &c.

		Dolls.	Cents.	Mills.
A †Farthing ...				4.1
4 Farthings = a penny ..			1	6⅔
12 Pence a shilling			20	
60 Pence a dollar		1		

	Dolls.	Cents.	Mill

CANADA, NOVA SCOTIA, &c.
(CONTINUED.)

		Dolls.		
20 Shillings = a pound		4		
30 Shillings a moidore . ..		6		
40 Shillings a half Joe . .		8		
50 Shillings a Federal Eagle .		10		

Accounts are kept in pounds, shillings and pence; but they are also kept in some parts of Canada in Livres, sous, and deniers, according to the ancient system of France, and is called *Old Currency.*

MEXICO, PERU, CHILI, &c.

☞ Accounts are kept here, and all other parts of Spanish America in Pesos and Dollars of 8 Reals, the Real being divided into halves and quarters: this Real is occasionally divided into 16 parts, and also into 34 Maravedis of Mexican plate.

BRAZIL.

Accounts are kept here as in Portugal, in Reas. 1000 making the Milrea; 100.000 being 100 milreas; and 1,000,000, one thousand Milreas, commonly called a *Conto* of Milreas.

EUROPE.

NORTHERN PARTS.

ENGLAND AND SCOTLAND.

London, Liverpool, Bristol, Ediuburg, Glasgow, &c.

	Dolls.	Cents.	Mill
A †Farthing .			4.6
2 Farthings = a halfpenny			9¼
2 Halfpence a penny.. . .		1	8½

ENGLAND AND SCOTLAND.	Dolls.	Cents.	Mills.
(CONTINUED.)			
4 Pence = a groat		7	4
6 Pence a half shilling		11	1 1
12 Pence a shilling		22	2.2
54 Pence an American dollar	1		
5 Shillings a crown	1	11	1.1
20 Shillings a pound sterling ...	4	44	4.4
21 Shillings an English guinea.....	4	66	6.7

Accounts are kept in Pounds, Shillings, Pence, and Farthings.

Note. Although the English crown at the par of exchange is $1 11 1 1, yet in the United States it passes only for $1 10 cents, and the gold coins, instead of passing at their par value, are now regulated by the rate of exchange between the two countries.

IRELAND.

Dublin, Cork, Londonderry, &c.

	Dolls.	Cents.	Mills.
A †Farthing			4.3
2 Farthings = a halfpenny			
2 Halfpence a penny			
12 Pence a shilling ...			
13 Pence an English shilling . .			
58½ Pence an American dollar ..			
20 Shillings a pound....			
22¾ Shillings an English guinea			

Accounts are kept in Pounds, Shillings, Pence, and Farthings.

BREMEN.

	Dolls.	Cents.	Mills.
A †Pfening.... ... . .,.....			1
2 Pfenings = a sware			2
5 Swares a grote. ; .		1	0.6

BREMEN.—(CONTINUED.)		Do'a.	C nts.	Milla.
3 Grotes = a double shilling			3	2
24 Grotes	a mark　..		25	5½
48 Grotes	a double mark　...		51	1
72 Grotes or				
3 marks	a †rixdollar　...:...		76	6½

Accounts are kept in Rixdollars and Grotes.

HANOVER.

Lunenburg, Zell, &c.

		Do'a.	C nts.	Milla.
A †Pfening.... .　...				2　7
3 Pfenings = a dreyer　.				8　2
8 Pfenings	a marien		2	1.9
12 Pfenings	a †grosh...		3	2.6
8 Groshen	a half guilden.		26	2½
16 Groshen	a guilden　.		52	5
24 Groshen	a †rixdollar .		78	7½
32 Groshen	a double guilden　..	1	5	
34 Groshen	a ducat.	1	10	

Accounts are kept in Rixdollars, Groshen, and Pfenings.

AUSTRIA AND SWABIA.

Vienna, Trieste, Augsburg. Blenheim, &c.

		Do'a.	C nts.	Milla.
A †Phening　.....			•	2..
2 Phenings = a dreyer　..				4
4 Phenings	a †creutzer			8¾
14 Phenings	.a grosh　.. .		3	0½
4 Creutzers	a batzen　... ,		3	5
15 Batzen	a †gould or †florin　.		52	5
90 Creutzers	a rixdollar.		78	7½

AUSTRIA AND SWABIA.
(CONTINUED.)

	Dolls.	Cents.	Mills.
30 Batzen = a specie dollar* ..	1	5	
60 Batzen a ducat	2	10	

Accounts are kept in Florins, Creutzers, and Phenings.

*Although the par of exchange makes a specie dollar 1 dollar and 5 cents, yet in the United States it is worth but a dollar.

OLLAND AND ZEALAND.

Amsterdam, Rotterdam, Middleburg and Flushing.

	Dolls.	Cents.	Mills.
A †Penning			1¼
8 Pennings = a grote..		1	
2 Grotes a †stiver		2	
6 Stivers a sealin		12	
20 Stivers a †guilder		40	
50 Stivers a rixdollar ..	1		
60 Stivers a drey guilder	1	20	
105 Stivers a ducat ..	2	10	
6 Guilders a pistole	2	40	

Accounts are kept in Guilders, Stivers, and Pennings.

EUROPE.

SOUTHERN PARTS.

PORTUGAL.

	Dolls.	Cents.	Mills.
A †Rea			1¼
10 Reas = a half vintin. ...		1	1½
20 Reas a vintin.		2	5
5 Vintins a testoon		12	5

	Dolls.	Cents.	Mills.
PORTUGAL.—(CONTINUED.)			
4 Testoons = a crusad of exchange.		50	
24 Vintins a new crusado ..		60	
10 Testoons a †millrea	1	25	
48 Testoons a moidore	6		
64 Testoons a Johannes	8		

Accounts are kept in Millreas and Reas.

FRANCE AND NAVARRE.

Paris, Lyons, Marseilles, Bordeaux, Bayonne, &c.

	Dolls.	Cents.	Mills.
A †Denier . . .			0¾
3 Deniers = a liard ..			2.3
2 Liards a dardene. .			4.6
12 Deniers a †sol . . .			9¼
20 Sols a †livre tournois .		18	5
60 Sols un ecu of exchange ·		55	5
6 Livres an ecu or crown	1	11	1 7
10 Livres a pistole	1	85	
24 Livres a Louis d'or	4	44	4.4

Accounts are kept in Livres, Sous, and Deniers.

Since 1795 accounts are kept in France of 10 Decimes or 100 Centimes. The Livre and Franc were formerly of the same value; but by a decree of 1810, the following proportion has been established :

Pieces of 48 Livres at 47f. 20c.

      of 24   at 23 55

      of 6   at 5.80

      of 3   at 2.75

The modern gold coins are Napoleons of 40 and 20 Francs, and Louis of the same weight and current value.

	Dolls.	Cents.	Mills.
Note. French crowns at the par of exchange are estimated at 1 dollar 11 1 1 cts., but they only pass for 1 dollar 10 cts.			

SPAIN AND CATALONIA.

Madrid, Cadiz, Seville, &c.

NEW PLATE.

		Dolls.	Cents.	Mills.
A †Maravedi				2.9
2 Maravedis = a quartil.				5.8
34 Maravedis	a †Real ...		10	
2 Reals	a pistareen		20	
8 Reals	a piastre of exchange		80	
10 Reals	a †dollar ..	1		
375 Maravedis	a ducat of exchange	1	10	2
32 Reals	a pistole of exchange	3	18	5
36 Reals	a pistole	3	72	2

Accounts are kept in Dollars, Reals, and Maravedis.

Gibraltar, Malaga, Denia, &c.

VELÓN.

		Dolls.	Cents.	Mills.
A †Maravedi...				1.6
2 Maravedis = an ochavo ∴				3.2
4 Maravedis	a quartil. ..			6.4
34 Maravedis	a †real velon ..			3.2
15 Reals	a †piastre of ex. .		79	6.3
512 Maravedis	a piastre. .		79	6.3
60 Reals	a pistole of ex. ...	3	18	5
2048 Maravedis	a pistole of ex.	3	18	5
70 Reals	a pistole .	3	72	2

Accounts are kept in Dollars, Reals, and Maravedis.

Barcelona, Saragossa, Valencia, &c.	Dolls.	Cents.	Mills.
OLD PLATE.			
A †Maravedi			3.9
16 Maravedis = a soldo...		6	2¼
2 Soldos a †rial, old plate ..		12	5
16 Soldos a †dollar	1		
20 Soldos a libra.	1	25	
24 Soldos a ducat :.∴	1	50	
60 Soldos a pistole.	3	60	

There are also Ducats of 21 and 22
Soldos.

Accounts are kept in Dollars, Reals
and Maravedis.

Note.—Although 60 Soldos are equal to
3 dollars and 75 cents, the Spanish Pistole
is worth but 3 dollars and 60 cents.

ITALY.

GENOA, *Novi,* &c., CORSICA, *Bastia,* &c.

	Dolls.	Cents.	Mills.
A †Denari			6¾
12 Denari = a †soldi. '			7.9
4 Soldi a chevalet		3	1.8
20 Soldi a †lira		15	9.2
30 Soldi a testoon		23	8½
5 Lires a croisade		79	6.3
115 Soldis a pezzo of exchange..		92	5.9
6 Testoons a genoine ...	1	44	4
20 Lires a pistole	8	18	5

Accounts are kept in Lires, Soldis, and
Denaris.

Leghorn, Florence, &c.

	Dolls.	Cents.	Mills.
A †Denari			0.0
4 Denaris = a quatrini ..			2.6

14

ITALY, &c.—(CONTINUED.)		Dols.	Cents.	Mills.
12 Denaris = a †Soldi	... ...	0		7 7
5 Quatrinis a craca	... ...			2.8
18 Craças a quilo	... ...			
20 Soldi a †lira	... ...		1	4.3
6 Lires a piastre of exchange	...		92	5.9
7½ Lires a ducat	... ...	1	15	
22 Lires a pistole	... ...	3	44	

Accounts are kept in Lires, Soldis, and
Denaris.

ASIA.

BENGAL.

Calcutta, Calliout, &c.

A †Pice	...			2.9
4 Pices = a fanum	.. ..		1	1 6
6 Pices a viz	...		1	7.3
12 Pices an ana	....		3	4.7
10 Anas a piano			34	6.8
16 Anas a rupee	...			
2 Rupees a French ecu or crown	...	1	1	1
2 Rupees an English crown	. .	1		
56 Anas a pagoda	...	1	94	4

A Lack is 100,000 rupees......

Accounts are kept in Rupees, Anas, and
Pice.

CHINA.

Pekin, Canton, &c.

A ††Cash	...			1.4
10 Cash = a †candareen	...		1	4.8
10 Candareens a †mace	...		14	8
10 Mace, 1 oz. 6 dwt. 16 grs. = a †tale	1	48	

Accounts are kept here in Tales, Mace,
Candareens, and Cash.

	Dolls.	Cents.	Mills.
Mocha.			
A †Carat....			2
5 Carats = a commarsee		1	
Carats a †caveer		1	0.4
Commarsees a coffala		6	6¾
Coffalas a †Mocha dollar		83	3.4
Mocha Dollar a Spanish Dollar	1		
Coffalas a sequin ...	1	66	6¾
Sequins a tomond	15		

Accounts are kept in Piastres or Mocha Dollars, and Caveers.

ε.
μ

ISLAND OF JAVA.

Batavia.

	Dolls.	Cents.	Mills.
A †Doit			4.2
4 Doits = a †stiver		1	6¾
8 Doits a cash or dubbettjees		1	6¾
3 Doits a satalie or schilling		10	
3 Satalies a sooka		20	
9 Cash a sooka satalies		30	
15 Cash a current rupee		50	
24 Cash a †Pardaoor rixdollar		80	
60 Stivers a dollar	1		
13 Schillings a ducatoon	1	30	

Note.—A new system of monies has been established by the king of the Netherlands.

The unit is the new Gulden or Florin of the Netherlands, and instead of decimal divisions is divided into 4 Schillings, 12 Dubbels, 24 Dutch Stivers, 30 Indian Stivers, or 120 Doits.

	Dolls.	Cents.	Mills.
Isle of Bourbon, and Isle of France.			
A Denier			0.4
12 Deniers = a †Sous			5
20 Sous a †livre		10	
10 Livres a dollar	1		

AFRICA.

EGYPT.

Old and New Cairo, Alexandria, Sayde, &c.

	Dolls.	Cents.	Mills.
An †Asper		1	0.3
3 Aspers = a †medino.. . . .		3	0.8
24 Medini an Italian ducat. :		74	
80 Aspers a piastre.		88	9
30 Medini a dollar .	1		
96 Aspers an ecu	1	10	
32 Medini a crown	1	10	
200 Aspers a suttanin	2	22	
70 Medini a Parzo dollar	2	33	

Accounts are kept in Piastres, Medini, and Aspers.

BARBARY.

Algiers, Tunis, Tripoli, Una, &c.

	Dolls.	Cents.	Mills.
An †Asper		1	0.8
8 Aspers = a medino.		3	9.8
10 Aspers a real, old plate.		12	5
2 Reals a †double		25	
4 Doubles a dollar . . .	1		
24 Medini a silver chequin.		74	
30 Medini a dollar	1		
180 Aspers a zequin	1	96	3
15 Doubles a Pistole	3	72	

Accounts are kept in Doubles and Aspers.

		Dolls.	Cents.	Mills.
WEST INDIES.				
Jamaica and Bermudas.				
A Farthing	.			3.1
4 Farthing =	a †penny ,		1	2½
7½ Pence	a real or bit		10	
2 Bits	a pistereen ..		20	
12 Pence	a †shilling		15	
20 Pence	a ¼ of a dollar ..		25	
80 Pence	a dollar .	1		
16 Shillings	a half English guinea	2	33	3 3
20 Shillings	a †pound .	3		
40 Shillings	a moidore ..	6		
53½ Shillings	a half joe, 9 dwt. ..	8		

Accounts are kept in Pounds, Shillings, and Pence.

Note.—As the currency of Jamaica is 1.40*l.*, its proportion to sterling is as 7 to 5. Hence 1*l.* sterling = 1*l.* 8*s.* currency; and 1*l.* currency = 14*s.* 3½*d.* sterling.

———

		Dolls.	Cents.	Mills.
Barbadoes.				
A Farthing .. , . ..				3.3
4 Farthings =	a penny .		1	3¼
7½ Pence	a real or bit		10	
2 Bits	a pistereen ..		20	
12 Pence	a shilling		16	
75 Pence	a dollar ... ... ,	1		
20 Shillings	a pound ..	3	20	
27½ Shillings	a moidore ..	6		
50 Shillings	a half Johannes	8		

Accounts are kept in Pounds, Shillings, Pence, and Farthings.

		Dolly.	Cents.	Mills.

Bahamas.

		Dolls.	Cents.	Mills.
A †Farthing				2 6
4 Farthings = a †penny			1	0½
9 Pence	a bit .		10	
12 Pence	a †shilling		12	5
96 Pence	a dollar.	1		
20 Shillings	a †pound	3		
48 Shillings	a moidore	6		
64 Shillings	a half Johannes	8		

Accounts are kept in Pounds, Shillings, Pence, and Farthings.

St. Bartholomews, St. Kitts, Nevis, Antigua and Montserrat.

		Dolls.	Cents.	Mills.
A †Farthing				2½
4 Farthings = a †penny			1	
9 Pence	a bit		9	
12 Pence	a †shilling		12	
8¼ Shillings	a dollar	1		
11 Bits	a dollar	1		
20 Shillings	a †pound	2	40	
66 Shillings	a half Johannes	8		

Money of account, Pounds, Shillings, Pence, and Farthings.

Dominica, St. Vincents, Grenada, St. Lucia, &c.

		Dolls.	Cents.	Mills.
A †Farthing				2.3
4 Farthings = a †penny				9¼
9 Pence	a bit		8	3.3
12 Pence	a †shilling		11	1.1

	Dolls.	Cents.	Mills.
Dominica, &c. (CONTINUED.)			
12 Bits = a dollar	1		
20 Shillings a †pound	2	22	2 . 2

Accounts are kept in Pounds, Shillings, Pence, and Farthings.

———

	Dolls.	Cents.	Mills.
Martinique, St. Lucia, Guadaloupe, &c.			
A Denier ..			0½
12 Deniers = a sol			5½
15 Sols an escalin		8	2 . 5
20 Sols a livre		11	1 1
3 Escalins a ¼ gourde. .		25	
9 Livres a piastre gourde ..	1		
12 Escalins a piastre gourde	1		
8 Gourdes a ½ johannes, 9 dwts. ..	8		
¼ of a Quadruple = 4 dwts. 6 grs..	4		
½ of a Quadruple 8 dwts. 12 grs.	8		
A Quadruple 17 dwts..	16		

Money of account, Livres, Sols, and Deniers.

———

	Dolls.	Cents.	Mills.
St. Domingo, (Spanish part,) *Cuba, Porto Rico, &c.*			
A Quarter Real		3	1¼
A †Half Real ..		6	2½
4 Quarters = a †real		12	5
2 Reals a Peso Medeo . .		25	
4 Reals a †peso or dollar .	1		

Accounts are kept in Pesos or Dollars, Reals, and Half Reals.

	Dolls.	Cents.	Mills
St. Domingo, (French part.)			

In the French part of St. Domingo or Hayti, accounts were formerly kept in Livres, Sols, and Deniers current; and the Dollar was then reckoned at 8 Livres 5 Sous current; but at present accounts are mostly kept in Dollars and Cents, as in the United States.

———

	Dolls.	Cents.	Mills
St. Eustatia, St. Martin, Curaçoa, &c.			
A Farthing .. .			2½
4 Farthings = a †penny.... ...		1	
9 Pence a bit		9	
12 Pence a †shilling....		12	
8½ Shillings a dollar	1		
11 Bits a dollar	1		
20 Shillings a †pound.	2	40	

Money of account, Pounds, Shillings, Pence, and Farthings.

———

	Dolls.	Cents.	Mills
St. Thomas, St. John, Santa Cruz.			
A †Stiver		1	3½
5 Stivers = an old Bit		6	6⅔
6 Stivers a †good bit		8	
8 Good Bits a †piece of ⅜ .		64	
12½ Good Bits, or 15 Old, a dollar ..	1		
75 Good Bits a moidore	6		
100 Good Bits a half joe....	8		

Accounts are made out in Pieces of ⅜, Bits, and Stivers.

	Dolls.	Cents.	Mills.
Surinam, Berbice, Demerara, &c.			
A †Duit			1¼
16 Duits = a stiver		3	
20 Stivers a guilder		40	
2½ Guilders a dollar	1		
5 Guilders ⅛ johannes	2		
15 Guilders a moidore.... .	6		
20 Guilders a half johannes ..	8		

Accounts are kept in Guilders, Stivers, and Duits.

———

	Dolls.	Cents.	Mills.
Canary and Madeira Islands.			
A †Ree			1
62½ Rees = a sixteenth of a dollar		6	2¼
62½ Rees ¼ of a pistareen ..		5	
125 Rees ⅛ of a dollar		12	5
125 Rees ½ of a pistareen		10	
250 Rees ¼ of a dollar		25	
250 Rees a pistareen ..		20	
1000 Rees a milree	1		

Accounts are kept, as in Portugal, in Rees and Milrees.

Note.—A pistareen, which is worth only 20 Cents, passes in Madeira, the same as a quarter of a Dollar, which is worth 25 Cents

SHORT METHOD

TO

·CALCULATE INTEREST.

RULE.

Multiply the sum by half the number of days,* that product being divided by 30 will give the interest in cents.

EXAMPLES.

What is the interest of 165 dollars for 16 days.

```
        165 dollars
          8 half the number of days
        ────────────
30)1320(44 cents
   120
   ────────
   120
   120
```

REDUCTION OF COINS.

The Dollar having different denominations of value throughout the United States, some simple rules for reducing the respective nominal values to Dollars and Cents may not be unacceptable.

The Dollar is valued at 6 Shillings in the states of New Hampshire, Massachusetts, Rhode Island, Connecticut, Virginia, Kentucky, and Tennessee.

To reduce the Currency of these States to Dollars and Cents, take this

RULE.

Add a cypher to the right hand of the pounds, and divide

---

* Counting 360 days in a year.

by 3, the quotient will be dollars—If there are shillings in the sum, add 1 dollar for every 6s.

EXAMPLES.

1. Reduce 100*l.* to dollars and cents.

$$3)1000$$

Answer $333⅓ or 33⅓ cents.

2. Reduce 46*l.* 15*s.* 9*d.* to dollars and cents.

$$3)460$$

$$153.33⅓$$

15*s.* = 2.50
9*d.*   12½

Answer $155.96 nearly.

The Dollar is valued at 7*s.* 6*d.* in the States of Pennsylvania, New Jersey, Maryland, and Delaware; to reduce which to Dollars, take the following

RULE.

Multiply the pounds by 8; dividing that product by 3, gives the dollars; and where there are shillings add one dollar for every 7*s.* 6*d.*

EXAMPLES.

Reduce 30*l.* 15*s.* to dollars and cents.

30   15*s.*

$$3)240$$

$$80$$

15*s.* = 2

Answer $82

The Dollar passes for 8 shillings in the States of New York and North Carolina; to reduce which to Dollars, use this

RULE.

Multiply the pounds by 2½, and the product will be dollars; and where there are shillings, add one dollar for every 8s.

EXAMPLES.

Reduce 30l. 12s. to dollars and cents.
$$30 \quad 12s.$$
$$2\tfrac{1}{2}$$

$$60$$
$$15$$
$$12s. = 1.50$$

Answer $76.50

In the States of South Carolina and Georgia, the Dollar passes for 4s. and 8d. to reduce which into Dollars, take this

RULE.

Add a cypher to the right hand of the pounds, then multiply by 3, and divide by 7, and the quotient is the dollars; and if there are shillings, add a dollar for every 4s. 8d.

EXAMPLES.

Reduce 10l. 10s. to dollars and cents
$$100$$
$$3$$

$$7)300$$

$$42.85.6$$
$$9s. \ 4d. = 2.$$
$$8s. \quad .14.2$$

Answer $45.00.0

A TABLE,

Exhibiting the standard weight, and Federal value of the Gold Coins, that pass current in the United States, with their value in the currencies of the respective States.

Names of Coins.	Standard Weight. (dwt. gr.)	Federal Money. (D. c. m.)	New England States, Virginia, Kentucky and Tennessee (L. s. d.)	New York and N. Carolina. (L. s. d.)	New Jersey, Pennsylvania, Delaware, and Maryland. (L. s. d.)	South Carolina & Georgia. (L. s. d.)
*Federal Coins.						
Eagle	11 6	10 00 0	3 0 0	4 0 0	3 15 0	2 6 8
Half Eagle.	5 15	5 00 0	1 10 0	2 0 0	1 17 6	1 3 4
Quarter Eagle.	2 19¼	2 50 0	0 15 0	1 0 0	0 18 9	0 11 8
Foreign Coins.						
Johannes	18 0	16 00 0	4 16 0	6 8 0	6 0 0	4 0 0
Half Johannes	9 0	8 00 0	2 8 0	3 4 0	3 0 0	2 0 0
Moidore	6 18	6 00 0	1 16 0	2 8 0	2 5 0	1 3 0
English Guinea	5 6	4 66 6	1 8 0	1 17 0	1 15 0	1 1 9
French Guinea.	5 5	4 56 2	1 7 6	1 16 0	1 14 6	1 1 5
French Pistole	4 5	3 64 9	1 2 0	1 8 0	1 7 6	0 17 6
Spanish Doubloon	17 8	15 18 2	4 8 0	5 16 0	5 12 6	3 10 0
Spanish Pistole.	4 8	3 79 5	1 2 0	1 9 0	1 8 0	0 18 0

*The Standard for Gold Coins of the United States is eleven parts fine, to one part alloy; Silver Coins 1485 parts fine, to 179 parts alloy.

TABLE

A TABLE,

Showing the number of days from any day in one month, to the same day in any other month. Very useful in Banking Business.

From	Jan.	Feb.	Mar.	April	May	Jun.	July	Aug.	Sept.	Oct.	Nov.	Dec.
January	365	31	59	90	120	151	181	212	243	273	304	334
February	334	365	28	59	89	120	150	181	212	242	273	303
March	306	337	365	31	61	92	122	153	184	214	245	275
April	275	306	334	365	30	61	91	122	153	183	214	244
May	245	276	304	335	365	31	61	92	123	153	184	214
June	214	245	273	304	334	365	30	61	92	122	153	183
July	184	215	243	274	304	335	365	31	62	92	123	153
August	153	184	212	243	273	304	334	365	31	61	92	122
September	122	153	181	212	242	273	303	334	365	30	61	91
October	92	123	151	182	212	243	273	304	335	365	31	61
November	61	92	120	151	181	212	242	273	304	334	365	30
December	31	62	90	121	151	182	212	243	274	304	335	365

Example.—Look for April at the left hand, and September at the top—in the angle is 153.

TABLE OF INTEREST,

Per day, at 6 per cent. on any number of Dollars, from One to Twelve Thousand.

Princip.	Interest.	Princip.	Interest.	Princip.	Interest.	Princip.	Interest.
D.	M.	D.	M.	D.	C. M.	D.	D. C. M.
1	013	51	510	61	1.203	91	1.496
2	033	52	526	62	1 019	92	1.512
3	049	33	542	63	1 036	93	1 529
4	066	34	559	64	1.052	94	1.545
5	082	35	575	65	1.068	95	1.562
6	099	36	592	66	1.085	96	1.578
7	115	37	608	67	1 101	97	1.595
8	132	38	625	68	1 118	98	1.611
9	148	39	641	69	1.134	99	1 627
10	164	40	658	70	1 151	100	1.644
11	181	41	674	71	1 167	200	3.288
12	197	42	690	72	1.184	300	4.932
13	214	43	707	73	1 200	400	6 575
14	230	44	723	74	1 216	500	8 219
15	247	45	740	75	1.233	600	9.863
16	263	46	756	76	1.249	700	11.507
17	279	47	773	77	1.266	800	13 151
18	296	48	789	78	1 282	900	14.795
19	312	49	808	79	1.299	1000	16.438
20	329	50	822	80	1.315	2000	32.877
21	345	51	838	81	1.332	3000	49 815
22	362	52	855	82	1 348	4000	65.753
23	378	53	871	83	1 364	5000	82 192
24	395	54	888	84	1 381	6000	98 630
25	411	55	904	85	1.397	7000	1.15.058
26	427	56	921	86	1.414	8000	1.31.507
27	444	57	937	87	1.430	9000	1.47.945
28	460	58	953	88	1 447	10000	1 64.384
29	477	59	970	89	1.463	11000	1.80.822
30	493	60	986	90	1.479	12000	1.97.260

A PRACTICAL SYSTEM

OF

BOOK-KEEPING,

FOR

FARMERS AND MECHANICS.

Almost all persons, in the ordinary avocations of life, unless they adopt some method of keeping their accounts in a regular manner, will be subjceted to continual losses and inconveniences; to prevent which the following plan or outline is composed, embracing the principles of Book-Keeping in the most simple form. Before the pupil commences this study, it will not be necessary for him to have attended to all the rules in the Arithmetic; but he should make himself acquainted with the subject of Book-Keeping, before he is suffered to leave school. A few examples only are given, barely sufficient to give the learner a view of the manner of keeping books; it being intended that the pupil should be required to compose similar ones, and insert them in a book adapted to this purpose.

Book-Keeping is the method of recording business transactions. It is of two kinds — single and double entry; but we shall only notice the former.

Single entry is the simplest form of Book-Keeping, and is employed by retailers, mechanics, farmers, &c. It requires a Day-Book, Leger, and, where money is frequently received and paid out, a Cash-Book.

———

DAY-BOOK.

This book should be a minute history of business transactions in the order of time in which they occur; it should be ruled with head lines, with one column on the left hand for post-marks and references, and two columns on the right for dollars and cents. The owner's name, the town or city, and the date of the first transaction, should stand at the head of the first page. It is the custom of many to continue inserting the name of the town on every page. This, however, is unnecessary. It is sufficient to write only the month, day, and year, at the head of each page after the first. This should be written in a larger hand than the entries.

On commencing an account with any individual, his place of residence should be noted, provided it is not the same as that where the book is kept. If it be the same, this is unnecessary. As it often happens that different persons bear the same name, it is well, in such cases, to designate the individual with whom the account is opened, by stating his occupation, or particular place of residence.

When the conditions of sale or purchase vary from the ordinary customs of the place, it should be stated. Every month, or oftener, the Day-Book should be copied or posted into the Leger, as hereafter directed. The crosses, on the left hand column, show that the charge or credit, against which they stand, is posted, and the figures show the page of the Leger where the account is posted. Some use the figures only as post-marks.

Every article sold on credit, except when a note is taken, should be immediately charged, as it is always unsafe to trust to memory. Also, all labour performed, or any transaction whereby another is made indebted to us, should be immediately entered on the Day-Book. If farmers and mechanics would strictly observe this rule, they would not only save many quarrels, but much money. In this respect, at least, follow the example of Dr. Franklin, who never omitted to make a charge as soon as it could be done. Never defer a charge till to-morrow, when it can be made to-day.

EDWARD L. PECKHAM. *Jan.* 1, 1840.

		$	c
1 +	*James Murray, Jr.* .... Dr.		
	To 1 gall. Lisbon wine $1,92		
	" 6 yds. Calico, a 37½ cts. 2,25		
	" 2 yds. Broadcloth, a $4.50 9,00		
		13	17
+	*Robert Hawkins,* Blacksmith. ...... Dr.		
	To 217 lbs. Iron, a 8 cts.	17	36
2 +	*Thomas Yeoman* .. .. :........ .. Cr.		
	By Cash	75	75
	————— 3 —————		
2 +	*Archibald Tracy,* Salem ... .. Dr.		
	To one piece Broadcloth, containing 29 yds., a $3 per yd.,		
	90 days' credit	87	00
2 +	*James Warren,* Wartland. Dr		
	To 1 cask Nails, 225 lbs., a 8 cts.	18	00
	Cr.		
	By 37 lbs Cheese, a 10 cts. $3.70		
	" 41 lbs. Feathers, a 70 cts. 28,70		
	Balance to be paid in Corn, at market price.	32	40

15*

		$	c
2 +	*Isaac Thomas,* Brattle Square .. .. *Dr.*		
	To 32 galls. Molasses, *a* 50 cts.........................	16	00

────────── 4 ──────────

2 +	*William Angell,* .. .. *Dr.*		
	To 300 lbs. Pork, at 7 cts. $21,00		
	" 30 bu. Corn, *a* 45 cts. 13,50		
		34	50

7	*Samuel Stone.... ... . Dr.*		
	To 50 lbs Harness Leather, *a* 30 cts. $15,00		
	" 7 Tons Hay, *a* $10 70,00		
		85	00

────────── 5 ──────────

	George Carpenter . .. . *Dr.*		
2 +	To 17 Brooms, *a* 12 cts. $2,04		
	" 7 lbs. Butter, *a* 20 cts. 1,40		
	" 4 lbs. Cheese, *a* 10 cts. .... ,40		
		3	84

	Jesse B. Sweet, ... *Dr.*		
3 +	To 1 hhd. Molasses, 58—6 = 32 galls., *a* 30 cts..........	27	60
	Cr.		
	By Cash	15	00

	Jesse Metcalf, ... *Dr.*		
3 +	To 20 Calf-Skins, *a* $5................... $100,00		
	" 50 Dried Hides, *a* $4.............. 200,00		
	60 days' credit.	300	00

	James Murray, Jr. .. .. *Cr.*		
1 +	By 20 bu. Corn, *a* 60 cts..................... $12,00		
	" 4 bu. Oats, *a* 40 cts. 1,60		
		13	60

────────── 6 ──────────

2 +	*James Warren* .... *Dr.*		
	To 24 bu. Corn, *a* 60 cts.	14	40

	Archibald Tracy. .. .. .. *Dr.*		
2 +	To 1 cord Wood $6,00		
	" 30 lbs. Feathers, *a* 70 cts. 21,00		
		27	00

	Robert Hawkins ... . *Cr.*		
1 +	By shoeing my Horse.................. $2,00		
	" " " Oxen 3,00		
		5	00

────────── 7 ──────────

	Samuel Stone.. .. .. Dr.		
2 +	To 2 yds. Broadcloth, *a* $4 .... $8,00		
	" 4 pr. Shoes, *a* $1............. 4,00		
		12	00

Jan 5, 1840.

		$	c
2+	**Thomas Yeomans** .. .. .. **Dr.** To 200 bu. Corn. a 70 cts.	140	00
	———————9———————		
3+	**Jessee B. Sweet**. . **Dr.** To 30 quintals Fish, a $3,75	112	50
3+	**George Carpenter** **Dr.** To 200 lbs. Cheese, a 8 cts.................... $16,00 " 1 firkin Butter, 76 lbs., weight of tub. 10 lbs.— 66, a 20 cts. 13,20	29	20
2+	**Archibald Tracy**. .. .. **Dr.** To 2 bbls. Flour, a $10........................ $20,00 " 25 bbls. Lard, a 10 cts. .... 2,50 " 3 bu. Salt, a 66 cts. 1,98	24	18
2+	**Isaac Thomas** .... **Dr.** To 50 yds. Calico, a 22 cts. .... $11,00 " 75 yds. brown Shooting, a 14 cts. 10,50	21	50
	Cr. By Order on Goodrich & Lord, for $12,80	12	80
3+	**Jesse Metcalf** .. .. **Dr.** To 500 pr. Men's Shoes, a 95 cts.	475	00
	———————10———————		
2+	**Thomas Yeomans** .. .... **Dr.** To 3 bbls. Flour, a $9,50	28	50
1+	**Robert Hawkins** ... . **Dr.** To 120 lbs. Blistered Steel, a 8 cts............... $9,60 " 100 lbs. Russia Iron, a 5 cts.................. 5,00	14	60
1+	**James Murray, Jr.** .. .. **Dr.** To 10 lbs. Sugar, a 11 cts. .... $1,10 " 20 lbs. Coffee, a 15 cts. .... 3,00 " 6 galls. Molasses, a 37 cts. 2,22	6	32
2+	**William Angell** : .. .. **Cr.** By 200 lbs. Lard, a 6 cts........... .... $12,00 " 350 lbs. Bacon, a 12 cts. 42,00	54	00

Jan. 9, 1840.

2 +	*James Hammond*	**Dr.**	$	c
	To 1 bbl. Flour	$10,00		
	" 3 bu. Corn, a 65 cts.	1,95		
	" 6 galls. Wine, a 1,25....................	7,50		
	" 3 lbs. Coffee, a 16 cts.	,48		
	" 4 bu. Salt, a 70 cts....................	2,80		
	" 1 lb. Y. H. Tea	1,25		
	" 14 lbs Sugar, a 12 cts.	1,68		
	" 3 yds. Broadcloth, a $,250	7,50		
	" 12 yds. Shirting, a 19 cts.	2,28		
			35	44

————— 13 —————

1 +	*James Murray, Jr.*	**Dr.**		
	To 6 lbs. Raisins, a 20 cts.	$1,20		
	" 5 galls. Currant Wine, a 75 cts.	3,75		
			4	95

LEGER.

This book is used to collect the scattered accounts of the Day-Book, and to arrange all that relates to each individual into one separate statement. The business of collecting these accounts from the Day-Book, and writing them in the Leger, is called *posting*. This should be done once a month, or oftener. Debts due from others, and entered upon the Day-Book, are placed on the side of *Dr.*; whatever is on the Day-book as due to another is placed on the side of *Cr.*

When an account is posted, the page of the Leger, in which this account is kept, is written in the left hand column of the Day-Book.

Every Leger should have an alphabetical Index, where the names of the several persons, whose accounts are kept in the Leger, should be written, and the page noted down.

When one Leger is full, and a new one is opened, the accounts in the former should be all balanced, and the balances transferred to the new Leger.

————

EXPLANATION OF THE LEGER, AND THE MANNER OF POSTING.

It will be seen that the name of *James Murray, Jr.*, stands first on the Day-Book; of course, we shall post his account first. We enter his name on the first page of the Leger, in a large, fair hand, writing *Dr.* on the left, and *Cr.* on the right. At the top of the left hand column, we enter the year, under which we write the month and day when the first charge was made in the Day-Book, and in the next column the page of the

Day Book where the charge stands. Theu, as there are several articles in the first charge, instead of specifying each article, as in the Day-Book, we merely say, *To Sundries*, and enter the amount in the proper columns. This charge being thus posted, we write the page of the Leger, viz., 1, in the left hand column of the Day-Book, and opposite to it a $+$, to show more distinctly that the charge is posted. We then pass a finger carefully over the names, till we again come to the name of *James Murray, Jr.*, which we find on the second page; but, as this is credit, we enter it on the credit side, with the date and page in their proper columns. We then enter the Leger-page and cross, as before, and then proceed again in search of the same name, until every charge and credit is transferred into the Leger. The next name is to be taken and proceeded with in the same way as the first; and so continue till all the accounts are posted.

As it is uncertain how extensive an account may be when once opened, it is better to take a new page for every name, until all the Leger pages are occupied. By this time, it is probable, several accounts will have been settled, we may then enter a second name on the same page, and so continue till all the pages are full.

Whenever any account is settled, the amount or the balance is ascertained, and the settlement entered in the Leger. The settlement may also be entered in the Day-Book; and many practice this, although it is not essentially necessary. But it is essentially necessary that one, if not both the books, should show how every account is settled, whether by cash, note, order, goods, or whatever way the amount or balance is liquidated.

N. B. In making out bills, the Leger is used as a reference to the charges in the Day-Book, which must be exactly copied.

FORM OF A LEGER.

Dr.			James Murray, Jr.					Cr.	
1829.				$	c	1829.			$	c
Jan. 1.	1		To Sundries,	13	17	Jan. 5.	2	By Corn and Oats,	13	60
" 10.	3		do.	6	32	" 15.		By Cash, to bal.,	10	84
" 13.	3		do.	4	95					
				$24	44				$24	44

Dr.			Robert Hawkins,					Cr.	
1829.				$	c	1829.			$	c
Jan. 1.	1		To Iron,	17	36	Jan. 6.	2	By Work,	5	00
" 10.	3		" Sundries.	14	60	" 12.		" Note, a 60 days,	26	96
				$31	96				$31	96

Dr.   *Thomas Yeomans.*   **Cr.**

1829.				$	c	1829.				$	c
Jan.	7.	2	To Corn,	140	00	Jan.	1.	1	By Cash,	75	75
"	10.	3	" Flour,	28	50	"	11.		" Check for bal.,	92	75
				$168	50					$168	50

Dr.   *Archibald Tracy.*   **Cr.**

1829.				$	c	1829.				$	c
Jan.	3.	1	To Broadcloth,	87	00	Apr.	2.		By Cash.	138	48
"	6.	2	" Sundries,	27	00						
"	9.	2	do.	24	48						
				$138	48						

Dr.   *James Warren.*   **Cr.**

1829.				$	c	1829.				$	c
Jan.	3.	1	To Nails,	18	00	Jan.	3.	1	By Sundries,	32	40
"	6.	2	" Corn,	14	40						
				$32	40						

Dr.   *Isaac Thomas.*   **Cr.**

1829.				$	c	1829.				$	c
Jan.	3.	1	To Molasses,	16	00	Jan.	9.	2	By Order,	12	80
"	9.	2	" Sundries,	21	50	"	20.		" Note, a 90 days,	24	70
				$37	50					$37	50

Dr.   *William Angell.*   **Cr.**

1829.				$	c	1829.				$	c
Jan.	4.	1	To Sundries.	34	50	Jan.	10.	3	By Sundries,	54	00
"	16.		" Cash,	19	50						
				$54	00						

Dr.   *Samuel Stone.*   **Cr.**

1829				$	c	1829.				$	c
Jan.	4.	1	To Sundries,	85	00	Jan.	30.		By Cash,	97	00
"	7.	2	do.	12	00						
				$97	00						

Dr.   *George Carpenter.*   **Cr.**

1829.				$	c	1829.				$	c
Jan.	5.	1	To Sundries,	3	84	Jan.	15.		By note, a 30 days	33	04
"	9.	2	do.	29	20						
				$33	04						

Dr   Jesse B. Sweet.   Cr.

1829.			$	c	1829.				$	c
Jan. 5.	1	To Molasses,	27	60	Jan. 5.	1	By Cash,		15	00
" 9.	2	" Fish,	112	50	" 20.		" Cash, to bal.,		125	10
			$140	10					$140	10

Dr.   Jesse Metcalf.   Cr.

1829.			$	c	1859.			$	c
Jan. 5.	2	To Sundries,	300	00	Apr. 7.	By his check,		775	00
" 9.	3	" Shoes,	475	00					
			$775	00					

Dr.   James Hammond.   Cr.

1829.			$	c	1829.			$	c
Jan. 12.	3	To Sundries,	35	44	Jan. 30.	By Order on Brown & Ives,		35	44

INDEX TO THE LEGER.

A   PAGE.
Angell, William 2

C
Carpenter, George............... 2

H
Hawkins, Robert............... 1
Hammond, James 3

M
Murray, James 1
Metcalf, Jesse 3

B   PAGE
Sweet, Jesse B. ....
Stone, Samuel 2

T
Thomas, Isaac 2
Tracy, Archibald 2

W
Warren, James 2

Y
Yeomans, Thomas 2

CASH-BOOK.

This book records the payments and receipts of cash.

It is kept by making cash Dr. to cash on hand and what is received, and Cr. by whatever is paid out.

At the end of every day or week, as may best suit the nature of the business, the cash on hand is counted, and entered on the Cr. side.

If there is no error, this will make the sum of the Dr. equal to that of the Cr. A balance is then struck, and the cash on hand carried again upon the Dr. side.

FORM OF A CASH-BOOK.

CASH.

Dr   *Cr.*

1827.			$	c	1827.		$	c
Jan. 1	To Cash on hand		637	50	Jan. 2	By rent of store for one quarter, paid Thomas Taylor,	62	50
2	" J. Thompson		37	94				
"	" Hart, paid acc't.		65	43				
3	" H. Palmer on note		127	28	4	" Paid note to R. Thacher,	127	83
4	" S. Snowdon		84	73				
5	" J. Mervin on acc't.		17	90	5	" Family expenses,	27	61
6	" S. Crane		100	90	6	" Merchandise bo't of T. Thamor,	614	27
"	Sales of Merchandise		311	18		Cash on hand,	550	65
			1382	86			1382	86
8	Cash on hand,		550	65				

Form of a Bill from the preceding Work.

MR. JAMES MURRAY

          To EDWARD L. PECKHAM, *Dr.*

1820.				$	c
Jan. 1.	To 1 gall. Lisbon Wine	$1,92			
"	" 6 yds. Calico, a 37½ cts.	2,25			
"	" 2 yds. Broadcloth, a $4,50...................	9,00			
				13	17
" 10	To 10 lbs. Sugar, a 11 cts.	1,10			
" "	" 6 galls. Molasses, a 37½ cts.	2,22			
" "	" 20 lbs. Coffee, a 15 cts.	3,00			
				6	32
" 12	" 6 lbs. Raisins, a 20 cts.	1,20			
" "	" 5 galls. Currant Wine, a 75 cts.	3,75			
				4	95
				24	44

                Cr.

" 5	By 20 bu. Corn, a 60 cts.	12,00			
" "	" 4 bu. Oats, a 40 cts.	1,60			
" 15	" Cash to balance	10,84			
	Errors excepted,			24	44

                         EDWARD L. PECKHAM.

     January 15, 1829.

2d Form.

MR. JESSE METCALF

          To E. L. PECKHAM, *Dr.*

1829.			$	c
Jan. 5.	To 20 Calf-Skins, a $5		100	00
" "	" 50 Dried Hides, a $4		200	00
" "	" 500 pr. Men's Shoes, a 95 cts.		475	00
	Received payment, by his check, on N. E. Bank.		$775	00

     April 7, 1829.   EDWARD L. PECKHAM.

No. 1.   *Negotiable Not*.

$78,50.   *May* 25, 1827.

On Demand, I promise to pay Claude Lorraine, or Order, Seventy-eight Dollars Fifty Cents, with Interest, for value received:

JAMES HONESTUS.

No. 2.   *Note payable to Bearer.*

$40.   *Sept.* 17, 1827.

Six months from date, I promise to pay A. B., or Bearer, Forty Dollars for value received.

SIMEON PAYWELL.

No. 3.   *Note by two Persons.*

$500.   *Oct.* 28, 1827.

For value received, we, jointly and severally, promise to pay C. D., or Order, on demand, Five Hundred Dollars, with Interest.

HORACE WALCOTT.
JAMES HART.

No. 4.   *Note at Bank.*

$150.   *Feb.* 25, 1819.

Ninety-five days from date, I promise to pay Thomas Andrews, or Order, at the Phœnix Bank, One Hundred and Fifty Dollars, for value received.

JOHN REYNOLDS

16

Remarks relating to Notes of Hand.

1. A negotiable note is one which is made payable to A. B. or order.—It is otherwise, when these words are omitted.

2. By *endorsing a note* is understood, that the person to whom it is payable writes his name on the back of it. . For additional security, any other person may afterwards endorse it.

3. If the note be made payable to A. B., or *order*, (see No. 1,) then A. B. can sell said note to whom he pleases, provided he endorses it; and whoever buys said note may lawfully demand payment of the signer of the note, and if the signer, through inability or otherwise, refuses to pay said note, the purchaser may lawfully demand payment of the endorser.

4. If the note be made payable to A. B., or *bearer*, (see No. 2,) then the signer only is responsible to any one who may purchase it.

5. Unless a note be written payable on some specific future time, it should be written *on demand;* but should the words *on demand* be omitted, the note is supposed to be recoverable by law.

6. When a note, payable at a future day, becomes due, it is considered on interest from that time till payed, though no mention be made of interest.

7. No mention need be made in a note of the *rate* of interest: that particular is settled by law, and may be collected according to the laws of the state where the note is dated. In some states it is 6 per cent.; in others, 7.

8. If two persons, jointly and severally, (see No. 3,) sign a note, it may be collected by law of either.

9. A note is not valid, unless the words for *value received* be expressed.

10. When a note is given, payable in any article of merchandise, or property other than money, deliverable on a specified time, such articles should be rendered in payment at said time, otherwise the holder of the note may demand the value in money.

Account with Interest.

MR. THOMAS I. SPENCER

To H. TISDALL, *Dr.*

1816—Nov. 1. To 3 yards Cloth, *a* $7,50 per yd..	$22,50
Dec. 2. " 6 galls. Wine, *a* 4,25 per gall.	25,50
1819—Jan. 1. " Balance of Interest	5,80

$53,80

Supra. *Cr.*

1817—Nov. 1. By Cash	$22,50
1819—Jan. 1. Ditto in full	31,30

$53,80

Jan. 1, 1819. H. TISDALL.

Receipt for Money on Account.

Received of James Wardell, Three Dollars on account.

SIMEON BRANDT.

. . . June 21, 1816.

A General Receipt.

Received of Jonathan Andrews, Fourteen Dollars in full of all accounts.

HORACE RITTER.

Dec. 31, 1827.

Receipt for Money paid on a Note.

Received of Leonard Temple, Seventy-two Pounds and Eleven Shillings, on his note for the sum of One Hundred and Seventy-two Pounds, and dated at Enfield, Oct. 27, 1826.

D. THOMAS.

Boston, August 27, 1828.

An Order for Money.

MESSRS. R. POTTER & Co.

    Pay James Thomas, or Order, Eleven dollars, and this shall be your receipt for the same.

SHEELAH SPENCER.

      Sept. 16, 1828.

An Order for Goods.

MR. ALBION N. OLNEY,

    Pay the Bearer Seventy-one Dollars, in Goods from your store, and charge

Your obedient servant,

Oxford, Dec. 31, 1827.   R. RAYNALL.

Note. A receipt given in full of *all accounts* cuts off accounts only; but a receipt given in full of *all demands* cuts off not only all accounts, but all demands whatever.

    An order, when paid, should be receipted on the back, by the person to whom it is made payable, or by some one duly authorised to sign for him; but when it is made payable to *bearer*, or to *A. B. or bearer*, it may be received by any one who presents it for payment.

THE END.

www.ingramcontent.com/pod-product-compliance
Lightning Source LLC
Chambersburg PA
CBHW022354020726
47500CB00002B/279